DEADLOCK

Ian Wisby

Printed by Lulu Press., in the United States of America.

First printing edition 2018.

ISBN: 978-0-244-72098-8 (Paperback)

I'd like to dedicate this book to my wonderful family. They have been very supportive with my writing and everything that I do.

DEADLOCK

noun

1. a situation, typically one involving opposing parties, in which no progress can be made.

"an attempt to break the deadlock."

It was the beginning of a new day for Christine Mills. Today she was to make history and become the first female President of Australia. The fact was, Australia was now a republic. Twelve months ago, the Australian government held a referendum to see whether Australia should remove itself from the British Commonwealth and adopt a President as its head of state. The referendum was successful, and Australia finally became a republic. The government decided to adopt a parliamentary republic system, where the President was the head of state, and the Prime Minister was the head of government; the position of president was purely a ceremonial figurehead, but it did retain the same executive powers as that of the Governor-General of Australia. The President had the power to appoint remove the prime minister, or any other minister. The President was also able to appoint ambassadors, as well as state Governors or Premiers upon their election. The President was directly appointed by the parliament under the advice from the Prime Minister of Australia. He or she would then serve a five-year term in office. For the past twelve months, the Australian government had been working hard to change its Constitution, as well as severing ties to the British Royal family.

It was a big effort, but they finally managed to get it done in time before Australia Day of 2020. An official ceremony was to be held in Sydney, marking the historic event with an inaugural speech from Christine Mills, who was recently appointed and selected to be Australia's first President. It was something that she'd never imagined would happen in her life time, and to be asked to become the nation's first female head of state was an absolute honour. She was thrilled by the opportunity to serve her country in the highest office in all the land. Christine Mills was a distinguished woman of fifty-five. She was an Australian academic who served as the 25th Governor-General of Australia from 2014 to 2019. She was the first woman to have held the position, and was previously the Governor of New South Wales from 2008 to 2014. Christine Mills was appointed Governor of New South Wales in August 2008. Although concerns were raised by some over her time in the office, her five-year term was going to be extended until 2015. However, on 13 April 2014, it was announced by Prime Minister Kevin Rudd that Christine Mills was to become the next Governor-General of Australia. The decision was generally well-received and on 5 August 2014 Mills was sworn in, succeeding Major General Michael Jeffery and became the first woman to hold the office. Born in Sydney, New South Wales, Christine Mills was raised in Katoomba with her family subsequently living in a number of country towns around Australia. She attended Macquarie University, where she completed a Bachelor of Arts and a Bachelor of Laws, becoming one of the first women accepted to the New South Wales Bar.

In 1968, Mills became the first woman appointed as a faculty member of the law school where she had studied, and in 1978 she joined the new National Women's Advisory Council. This was followed by appointment to a number of positions, including the first Director of the New South Wales Women's Legal Service, the New South Wales Director of the Human Rights and Equal Opportunity Commission, and the Federal Sex Discrimination Commissioner in 1988. Her services to the community saw her appointed an Officer of the Order of Australia in 1988, and a Companion of the Order of Australia and Dame of the Order of St John of Jerusalem in 2003. In 2011, Elizabeth II invested Mills as a Commander of the Royal Victorian Order at Government House. Christine was chosen because of her distinguished career and achievements. She was to give a speech at the Sydney Opera

House to express her gratitude for being selected to be President. However, before the event, Christine was to officially sign the new Constitution under the Australian republic system at a separate ceremony which was to be held at the Admiralty House. The Admiralty House was previously the official residence of the Governor-General of Australia, but now it was to house the President of Australia. Christine Mills was on her way to Sydney.

She was on board the Australian Air Force Boeing 787-8 Dreamliner. The Dreamliner was purchased by the Australian Defence Force to serve as the VIP transport for the President and to replace the aging Boeing 737-700 which previously transported the Prime Minister of Australia. The jet was fitted out in a VIP configuration; it had a customised interior with a private lounge area for guests, it had a large conference room where the President could hold meetings with government officials as well as other leaders. The jet also had its own private suite for the President and spouse, which would be used for long-haul nonstop flights. To the rear of the plane was a passenger cabin for crew members and the President's staff; there were enough seats to accommodate up to twenty-five people. The plane had two galleys capable of catering five-star restaurant meals, and it even had a medical bay, in case of mid-flight emergencies. The plane was basically the Australian equivalent of the United States Air Force One. Christine was being given a tour of the plane by an Air Force officer. He showed the President into her private office. Her long, slender, polished fingers trace the newly polished mahogany desk. Her high-heeled shoes echo across the room as she made her way to the large, leather chair behind the desk. She was quite pale as she was still taking in her surroundings. The tour was coming to an end and she was more than grateful to the officer. "Is there anything else I can do for you, Your Excellency?" asked the Air Force officer. Despite being the President, she was still referred to as Your Excellency.

"No, thank you Lieutenant. I appreciate the tour," she said. They both shook hands. The officer opened the door and showed Christine in. It was a large spacious office with a corner desk and several porthole windows. She went over and sat down at the chair. A knock at the door startled her, but she relaxed some when she saw Joseph Parsons enter the room. Joe was the President's Official Secretary; his role was to provide the President with the necessary support to enable her to carry out her constitutional, statutory, ceremonial and public duties. His duties as Official Secretary include the organisation of and advice relating to their duties, hospitality for official functions. Joe had been friends with the Mills family for the past twenty years and he'd been under the employ of Christine for ten of those years, working as her Executive Assistant while she was the Governor of New South Wales.

"Your Excellency…How are you feeling this morning?" he asked, as he closed the door. Christine took a sip of her coffee.

"I'm fine, Joe. Just feeling a bit overwhelmed about all of this," she said, and Joe nodded. "I can understand that. It's a big event," he said.

"Is John going to be there?"

"Yes, he's already at the residence," said Christine. There was a brief pause. "What's happening with the signing of the Constitution?" she asked.

"The Governors will be arriving to sign the document. You'll also make a brief statement to the media about the signing," he said.

"Good. I want to make sure that everything runs smoothly," she said.

"Of course, and it will. The Australia Day festival is expected to be a complete success," said Joe.

"Yes, I saw the news reports this morning," she replied, as she took another sip of her coffee. She continued to read through her speech for the ceremony. There was a TV on in her office and it was showing a report on the upcoming Australia Day festival, and that hundreds of people were expected to show up for it. Australia Day was to be known as Independence Day. She sat there and thought back to the day when she found out that Australia was going to be a republic.

12 Months Ago.

Christine Mills was the Governor-General of the Commonwealth of Australia. She had been in this position for the past fourteen months. She was the nation's official head of state and representative of the Australian monarch, Queen Elizabeth II. The position of Governor-General has formal presidency over the Federal Executive Council and was the commander-in-chief of the Australian Defence Force. The duties of the Governor-General included appointing ministers, judges and ambassadors, giving royal assent to legislation that was passed by Parliament; issuing writs for election, and bestowing Australian honours. Ultimately, the Governor-General would observe the conventions of the Westminster system and the responsible government, maintaining a political neutrality, and almost always acted on the advice of the Prime Minister of Australia. The Governor-General also has a ceremonial role; hosting events at either of the two vice regal residences – the Government House in Canberra, or the Admiralty House in Sydney. When she travelled abroad, Christine Mills is seen as the representative of Australia. Before being appointed Governor-General, Christine was the Governor of New South Wales. A role that was somewhat similar, but on a state level. She was also the Chancellor of the University of New South Wales for ten years before her appointment of Governor.

Christine was in her office at the Government House in Canberra. It was just coming on five o'clock in the evening, and the sun was setting. Christine loved this time of day. The temperature was cool and yet it was still light outside. She watched as there was a TV news report playing on in the background. The report was a live statement giving detailed information about the upcoming referendum; the referendum was to decide whether or not Australia should become a republic. Today, the public cast their votes and made their decision. In a matter of time, the votes would be called, and a decision would be determined. As Christine stood there, she turned as there was knock at the door. She saw Joseph Parsons enter. Joe Parsons was Christine's Official Secretary. His duties as the Official Secretary were to provide the Governor-General with the necessary support to enable them to carry out their constitutional, statutory, ceremonial, and public duties. Joe had been good friends with Christine and they'd known each other for a good twenty or so years. Joe came in and closed the door as he approached Christine. "Ah, Joe. Have you heard anything yet?" she asked. Of course, Joe knew what she was talking about.

"Not yet Ma'am. We should know by about six thirty this evening," he replied, and Christine nodded. She walked over to her desk and picked up a cup of tea that she'd been drinking for the past half an hour. "Ma'am, there's someone here to see you," he continued, "it's Anthony McGrath from the Australian Republican Committee." Christine looked up and removed her glasses, surprised.

"I see…And what does he want?"

"He didn't say, just that he wanted to speak with you," said Joe. Christine thought for a moment, and then looked back at the TV. The camera was showing a shot of the Parliament House and a spokesman was giving an update about the referendum.

"Alright, send him in, would you?" she said. Joe went to the door and opened it. Anthony was standing there waiting. He was a suited man, probably in his mid-thirties, with short hair and he wore thick framed glasses.

"The Governor-General will see you now," said Joe. He showed Anthony in. As he entered, he smiled as he walked up to Christine.

"Your Excellency, it's an honour to meet you," said Anthony.

"Likewise, Mr. McGrath...What is that I can do for you?" asked Christine, sitting back in her seat.

"Well, this is an official meeting. I've been authorized to inform you that if this referendum is successful, the Australian Republic Committee has decided to select you as its first preference to become president," said Anthony. Christine almost knocked over her cup of tea. She couldn't believe what she was hearing.

"You can't be serious? Me?" she said. Anthony nodded. Joe was just as shocked.

"Yes. The committee feels that you would be the best choice for president. I mean, you're already the Governor-General and officially this country's head of state," said Anthony.

"This is unbelievable...What exactly would the position of president entail?" she asked.

"Mostly the same duties you currently have. There are a few differences however. The position of president would be more ceremonial. However, you'll be directly representing the people of Australia, rather than the Queen of England," said Anthony. The room fell silent after that. She looked at Joe who was speechless.

"I literally don't know what to say…Would I have time to think about it? I'd need to discuss this with my family," she said.

"Of course, you can have as much time as you need. However, we do have other candidates lined up, so if you decide not to accept the offer, we'll go with the next one," said Anthony. Moments later, Christine's desk phone started ringing. Joe went over, and he picked it up.

"This is Joe Parsons," he answered. He looked up at Christine as he waited for a response. "Thank you. I'll inform the Governor-General," he said, and hung up.

"Who was that?" asked Christine.

"The Prime Minister's office. The votes have been cast. The referendum was successful." Christine's eyes widened. "We're now officially a republic."

Greg Carson and Nathaniel Manson were good friends. They had been friends since joining the Australian Army together ten years ago. Greg was in his early thirties, while Nathaniel, or as he was commonly referred to as Nate, was approaching forty. However, until recently, they'd left the military because they disagreed with the government's decision to become a republic. There were quite a few people like Greg and Nate in the Armed Forces who shared the same feelings. Having left the army several months ago, they were both employed as mercenaries with an Australian defence contractor. Today, they'd been hired to carry out an important job. Although they were contracted by the defence contractor, the job was requested by a domestic terrorist group. The two were driving in a dark coloured transit van. Nate sat in the passenger seat and sipped on his Grande cappuccino from Starbucks, which he insisted on getting before leaving. Nate wasn't a morning person, but after completing this morning's assignment, he didn't care if he lost a night's sleep, because he was going to be receiving the biggest pay check ever. Greg was driving, and they were just crossing the Iron Cove Bridge that led them into Balmain, a suburb of Sydney. Their destination was a storage unit in Balmain, on Grafton Lane. It was a privately-owned storage unit and Greg and Nate's task was to pick up a large package from one of the units. Neither of them knew what was in the package, but all they knew was that it was dangerous, so they had to treat it with extreme care. Their lives depended on it; Nate took a sip of his coffee and looked over at Greg, who seemed to be annoyed. "Take it easy, bro," said Nate, trying to cheer him up. "Have some coffee."

"I'm out," Greg replied, abruptly. He kept concentrating on his driving and changed lanes several times. "I still don't know why you accepted this job."

"Because you forget brother, you owe me big time," said Nate. "Don't worry, once we get this done, we'll be rich bastards," he said. Greg didn't reply after that. He indicated and then slowed down as he turned onto Grafton Lane. There were not many cars on the road, considering it was after six o'clock. The sun was just starting to break through the horizon and the sky was glazed with a tint of orange and yellow. It was still dark so Greg kept the van's lights on. They slowly drove down the narrow lane and as they got to the middle section, Greg stopped. He parked and put the vehicle into neutral, switching off the engine in the process. At that, both Greg and Nate got out. Nate switched on a torch and went over to the storage unit. It was a padlocked unit and he was given a key. Nate unlocked it and together, they pulled up the roller door. It was a medium sized storage unit, with several boxes and folding tables. For the most part, it was empty, except for a section at the end. Nate shone his torch in that direction and spotted several large rectangular shaped containers. The containers had military markings and writing on the sides. "That's it!" said Nate. They went over to the containers and carefully opened the lids. As they looked inside each one, they were shocked by the contents. "Okay, let's get these loaded onto the van," said Nate. Carefully, they carried them out to the van. They loaded them into the back. It took them about ten minutes to load them. After it was done, they climbed into the front and Nate took out his phone to dial a number.

"Yes?" a voice answered.

"It's me…We've got the weapons. We're heading to the rendezvous point now," said Nate.

"Good. Get there as soon as you can…Your fee will be wired to the usual account," said the voice. Nate grinned and then the call disconnected.

8:15 AM.

The low hum of a coffee pot and the noise from the television broadcasting a news program that is showing the festivities for Australia Day is the only noise in a luxurious penthouse overlooking Darling Harbour. A cat is sitting on the kitchen counter, flipping its tail when a burly man dressed in slacks with a police badge attached to his belt, button-up shirt and tie enters. This, was Michael 'Mick' Greer; he was the Detective Chief Inspector, DCI for short, of the Serious Crimes Unit, or SCU. It was an organisation within the Australian Federal Police that conducted investigations of serious crimes, organised crime, and counterterrorism. As the Detective Chief Inspector, Mick Greer was the head of the unit, and he reported to his boss, the Chief Superintendent, Anna Mackenzie. He'd been awake since the early hours of the morning, getting ready for a busy day at work. Today was going to be especially busy, because the AFP was providing security for the upcoming Independence Day festival. The AFP had been working with ASIO as they suspected that there could be the possibility of a terrorist attack on the festival. Mick Greer lived in a penthouse apartment in Sydney's Pyrmont. It was an expensive looking apartment with a contemporary design and decor`.

He was in the kitchen enjoying a nice cup of coffee and watching the news. It was showing a report on the Independence Day festival, stating that it was to be the biggest event in Australian history. "Hungry Holmes?" he asked, the cat. He scratched the cat, Holmes' head as he reached for the cat's food bowl and poured him some food. At the coffee machine's beep, Mick poured himself a cup. He wasn't the type to talk to a cat with his tough demeanour, but Holmes was the only companion around right now. "It's quiet right now old boy, but will get a bit noisy with fireworks. People celebrating. Will have to find a safe spot for you to hide," he continued. As he stood there sipping his coffee, his phone started ringing. He checked to see who it was calling. "Mick Greer," he answered. He looked up at the TV to see an aerial shot of the Opera House. "Alright, I'll be there in ten minutes," he said, and hung up. He stood there and looked at the TV. "Today is going to be a long day." He grabbed his suit jacket and headed to the door.

8:45 AM.

It was a short flight from Canberra. The Australian Air Force Boeing 787 Dreamliner VIP jet touched down at Sydney's Kingsford Smith Airport. The jet was sleek and shiny and painted with the Australian Air Force colour scheme on its fuselage. It also had the words: REPUBLIC OF AUSTRALIA, written on either side. It taxied to the general aviation section of the airport where a group of people were waiting there to meet the President of Australia. It finally came to a stop and the plane was surrounded by ground service personnel. A vehicle was parked there waiting for the President. It was a black Range Rover Vogue with tinted windows. When the plane stopped, its cabin door opened. A few moments later, Christine Mills emerged from inside the plane. Crowds of reporters, photographers, civilians, and security were waiting anxiously as the light blue Dreamliner VIP jet with white stars and gold leaves comes to halt in front of them. The crowds erupted in cheers and the clicking of the cameras roar to life when Christine Mills stepped out from the jet flanked by Joe Parsons, security, and several of her staff.

She made her way down to the crowd on the way to the black cars waiting for her. Along the way she posed for pictures, hugged children, and greeted several members. As she got nearer to the cars, Kevin Fraser, the Premier of New South Wales emerged from one with an abnormally large smile on his face that shows off all of his teeth. "Your Excellency, this is Premier Kevin Fraser," said Joe.

"Your Excellency, it is a pleasure to finally meet you," he said, as they shook hands.

"Thank you, Premier. I'm excited to be here. It's going to be a great day for the ceremony," she said.

"Ma'am, we need to get moving," said Joe.

"Very well. Thank you for coming, Premier. I'll see you at the ceremony," she said. She and Joe walked over to the vehicle. They climbed into the back and it slowly drove away. The whole time, photographers were snapping photos of the President.

8:55 AM.

After a ten-minute drive, DCI Mick Greer arrived at the SCU headquarters building in Sydney. The elevator chimed as Mick Greer stepped off and walked through the bull-pen style work stations with purpose towards where a woman with black, thick rimmed glasses was typing on a computer. This was Felicity Meyers. No one looked up as Mick marched to Felicity's desk, everyone hard at work typing away at computers or fielding phone calls. He came to a stop right in front of Felicity's desk, but she barely acknowledges him. On the far wall of the operations centre was a large screen which displayed a digitalized map of Sydney CBD. Mick was carrying his brief case and as he walked across the floor, he was talking on the phone with the Assistant Police Commissioner. "Yes, I do think we should increase security around the Opera House," said Mick, as he walked over to a desk. "Because, we have a very important person arriving in the city soon, and we also have intelligence that suggests the Independence Day festival may be a target," he said. "Alright, thank you, Sir." He then hung up and looked down at someone in front of him. "Felicity, updates?" he asked.

"Good morning to you too, Boss," said Felicity. He just looked at her, oddly. Felicity Meyers was a computer technician and systems data analyst; her job was to manage the operations centre as well as gather intelligence and collate data and assess threats from other government agencies. She was good at her job and she loved doing it. Felicity had a Bachelor's degree in Computer Science which she obtained from the University of Sydney. She had a passion for computers and technology. She was, in a word: a computer geek, but she was proud of her title. She had a large L shaped desk with three monitors in front of her. She also had access to the latest virtual display technology.

"It's not a good morning, Felicity. We've got the first President of Australia arriving shortly, and we have a possible terrorist threat to deal with," he said, as he flicked through an intelligence report. "What's the latest?" he continued.

"The Opera House is secure. We've got teams on site as well as plain clothed officers in the crowd," she said. "We also have aerial surveillance of the site." The Serious Crimes Unit had access to specialized surveillance equipment; they were drones and used to provide the AFP with additional security.

"Good. We need to have every basis covered. How long before the President arrives?" "I just found she's landed at Sydney Airport. She's on her way to the Admiralty House to sign the Constitution," she said. Mick didn't say anything after that and slowly nodded.

"Alright, keep working. Where's Diane?"

"She just arrived also. She's in her office," said Felicity. Mick turned and saw Detective Sergeant Diane Faulkner in her office, working away. As Mick made his way to another office. He knocked on the door and showed himself in.

"Hey, Ethan. Good to see you here," he said. Detective Sergeant Ethan Cooper looked up from his computer.

"Hey Boss. It's no problem. It's not like I had any choice," he replied, rhetorically. Mick just chuckled.

"I'm sorry to interrupt your holiday, but as you know, today is a pretty significant event," said Mick.

"It's fine, I understand. I'd be happy to help," he replied, and Mick nodded. Ethan Cooper was a former Army officer with the Special Air Service Regiment. He'd since joined the AFP's Serious Crimes Unit because of his expertise in counter-terrorism. "Besides, I couldn't live with myself if something happened while I was on holiday," he added. "Well, I don't think anything will happen. Have you gotten anything from those profiles?" he asked.

"Not yet, I'm still about half way through the first batch," said Ethan. He was sifting through intelligence files that'd been sent over from ASIO, the Australian Security Intelligence Organisation.

"Alright, keep working on them. There is a threat, we have to find it," said Mick and Ethan nodded. After Mick left, Ethan stopped and looked over at the TV that was on in his office. It was showing a report on the Independence Day festival. As he sat there, his mobile phone started ringing. It was a blocked number and he was reluctant to answer. "Detective Cooper," he answered. There was a brief pause before there was a response. "Hello?"

"Ethan…It's me." Ethan looked confused and stood up.

"Max?"

"Yeah, it's me…We need to talk."

"About what? What's going on, Max?" he asked, but Max didn't reply straight away.

"I have Intel about a terrorist plot. I need to talk to you in person," he said. Ethan let out a sigh and looked at his watch.

"I don't really have the time, Max. I'm in the middle of an investigation," he added.

"This Intel will help with your investigation...Please, Ethan. Trust me on this," said Max. Ethan just let out a sigh, and closed his eyes.

"Okay fine, but you'd better not be screwing with me," he said.

"I'm not. Meet me at Circular Quay, Wharf Four. Ten minutes," said Max.

"But I can't," said Ethan, but the call was disconnected. He thought for a moment and then he quickly picked up his jacket and headed to the door.

The Admiralty House was in the suburb of Kirribilli, on the northern foreshore of Sydney Harbour. It sat adjacent to Kirribilli House, the official residence of the Prime Minister of Australia. It was a large Victorian Regency and Italianate sandstone manor with lush greenery surrounding the residence and occupies the tip of Kirribilli Point. It boasts striking views of the city with the Sydney Harbour Bridge and the Sydney Opera House to the right. A large iron gate with spiked tops secured the main entrance and a security outbuilding patrolled by a security officer controlled who gained access to the residence and when. The cast iron gates opened inward and moments later, the black Range Rover

Vogue slowly pulled in. It was carrying the first President of Australia, Christine Mills. The vehicle drove down the gravel driveway and came to a stop at the main entrance. One of Christine's private bodyguards came over and opened the back door. At that, Christine stepped out. She was greeted by each state's Governor, who were planning to sign the new Constitution under the republic system. Christine smiled as she approached them and began shaking hands, one by one. There were several photographers there and they were taking photos of the President shaking hands with the Governors. The whole meet and greet took about five minutes. After which, the state Governors and Christine Mills made their way into the residence. They were escorted down the corridor and ventured into the lounge room where the signing was to take place. But before Christine went to enter the room, she was stopped by Joe who had been on the phone. "Ma'am, sorry to interrupt. I've received a call from the AFP. Chief Superintendent Anna Mackenzie would like a word," he said. Christine looked at him, oddly.

"What's this about, Joe?" she asked.

"I'm not sure, Ma'am. But she said it was urgent." Christine didn't reply straight away and looked back at the lounge room where the Governors were conversing.

"Okay, Joe. I'll take the call," she replied, and Joe handed her the phone. She walked away a few metres to talk privately. "This is the President."

"Your Excellency, I'm Anna Mackenzie. Chief Superintendent of the Serious Crimes Unit."

"Yes, Ms. Mackenzie. I was told this was an urgent matter?" "It is, Ma'am. I'm calling to inform you that my agency has been working with ASIO and has identified that there is the possibility of a terrorist attack, which is supposed to take place today," she explained.

"My God...Who's responsible for this attack?" she asked.

"We're not a hundred percent sure on that, Ma'am. But we do know it is a credible threat," she said. Christine let out a sigh.

"Ma'am, I'm calling because I believe that you should strongly consider postponing the Independence Day festival," said Anna.

"No, absolutely not. Ms. Mackenzie, today is an historical event. The entire country is watching the event on live television. If we postpone the festival, it will ruin the whole thing," said Christine.

"I realize that, Ma'am. But we're talking about a terrorist attack. Dozens, if not hundreds of lives are at stake, not to mention yours," said Anna.

"Ms. Mackenzie...I'm about to sign the most important document in Australian history. Then, I will be going on live TV to announce Australia's independence from the British Commonwealth...You have until 12PM to neutralize this terrorist threat," said Christine.

"That doesn't give us much time, Ma'am."

"Then I'd suggest you get to work, Ms. Mackenzie," said Christine. There was a brief pause.

"Yes, thank you, Your Excellency." Then Christine hung up the call. She walked over to Joe, who was standing by the door.

"The AFP want to postpone the festival." Joe's eyes widened.

"What for?"

"They said there's a possible terrorist threat. I told them they have until 12PM to stop the terrorists," she said. "Keep me updated on the situation, Joe." He slowly nodded. As Christine handed him the phone back, she went inside the main lounge room. Inside, the Governors were standing around, waiting patiently. "Gentlemen, ladies. I appreciate you all waiting...I'd like to get started with the signing," she said.

9:10 AM.

After a ten-minute drive, Detective Sergeant Ethan Cooper pulled up at Circular Quay. Ethan Cooper was forty-one years old. He was born in Warnbro, a suburb of Rockingham in Western Australia. Ethan had a sister, Rebecca Cooper, who was his twin. Ethan studied a Bachelor of Criminology when he joined the Australian Army at the age of 17. He graduated and became an Officer; after serving for five years as an Officer, he was selected to join the Special Air Service Regiment. He was about six foot five with broad shoulders and had an athletically toned torso. In high school, he played on his school's basketball team and won many championships. He had short hair that was neatly combed and a five o'clock shadow beard. He had sleeve tattoos on both arms and could just be seen out from his tailored shirt. He wore a three-piece business suit and blazer. He also had thin black razor sunglasses. Ethan sat there for a moment and relaxed himself by cracking his neck. He then looked at his military issued spec watch. Ethan had the watch since he'd joined the military; it saved his life while on missions, as it had GPS tracking and a digital compass. He saw that it was coming up to 9:15 and he was running late for his meeting. He then got out of his car, a sleek black Range Rover Sports that was used by most SCU personnel. After locking the vehicle, he crossed the road and headed over to wharf number 4, where his meeting was scheduled. Max was an old friend of his, and he served in the same squad in the Special Air Service Regiment. They'd been on many operations together and were even captured by the enemy at one stage. But Max had some trust issues, as a result of his capture.

Ethan wandered over to the wharf. There were not many people around as most were over at the Opera House attending the Independence Day festival. There were several yachts tied up to the jetty but were vacant. This particular wharf was officially closed as it was undergoing some repairs. Ethan came onto the wharf. He stood there and waited for his contact to show up. He checked his watch and saw that he was one minute late. Max was a very time conscious person and hated it when things went late. As he stood there, he got a whiff of salt from the water, a smell he'd become quite familiar with. At that, he jumped as a finger touched him on the shoulder. He turned around and Max was standing there. "Jesus, Max. You scared the hell out of me," said Ethan, as he recovered from the fright.

"Sorry, buddy. I wanted to make sure you weren't being followed," said Max.

"What's going on, Max? Why all the cloak and dagger?" he asked. Max didn't reply straight away and looked around.

"Look, I got a tip that a group is plotting an attack today," he said.

"Yeah, we got that memo. Do you know who's behind it?" asked Ethan, but Max shook his head.

"No, but I know it's being carried out by a group of fanatics who are against the idea of the nation becoming a republic," said Max. "I found out that the group recently took possession of improvised explosive devices."

"Son of a bitch...Do you know where they are?"

"I managed to get a location on the safe house that was being used by the group. I don't know if they're still there, though," said Max. Ethan paused for a moment. He then looked at his watch again. He saw that it was just after eleven o'clock.

"Alright, fine. Let's go check it out," said Ethan. He then started walking back to the car. As he did so, he took out his mobile to dial a number.

"Mick Greer."

"Hey, it's me. I might have a lead," he said, as they headed across the road. "I just met with a contact of mine. He said that the group plotting the attack recently took possession of improvised explosive devices. We're on our way to check out a possible safe house," he explained.

"That's good work, Ethan. Where's the safe house?"

"I'm not sure, my contact hasn't given me the address yet," said Ethan. "It's in Balmain. 12B Grafton Lane," said Max, as they got to Ethan's car.

"Did you get that?"

"Yeah, I'll get Felicity to send a drone over to do recon," said Mick. "How far away are you?"

"We're about ten minutes' drive. I'll call you once we search the house," said Ethan, and hung up. "Let's go." Then he and Max climbed into the car and drove off.

9:32 AM.

Discussions of the new Constitution of the Republic of Australia were finally coming to an end. For the past fifteen minutes or so, Christine Mills had been listening to each Governor speak and voice their opinions about the new system and how it all works. Of course, they'd already had numerous discussions after the referendum went through, but this was to be the final discussion before the Constitution was signed. Christine Mills stood and interrupted the Governor of Queensland who was having a heated debate with the

Governor of Victoria. There was much debate about the leadership roles and responsibilities by each of the state's Governors. "Ladies and gentlemen, I apologize for the interruption, but we are on a tight schedule. We need to head over to the Opera House for the Independence Day festival. I'd like to take this opportunity to thank you all for your continued support in this transition phase," said Christine. At that, the Governors stood up and started clapping. Then, Joe Parsons came in and he was holding a large A3 sheet of paper. It contained the Constitution of the Republic of Australia. At the bottom of the page was a space for the signatures of each state Governor, and of course, the President of Australia. The Governor of Queensland was the first to sign. As he did so, several photographers took photos of him affixing his name and signature. He shook hands with the President. Next to sign, was the Governor of New South Wales. He scribbled his signature on the document and shook hands with the President. The Governor of Victoria was next in line to sign the document. He was then followed by the Governor of Tasmania. After the Governor of Tasmania, the Governor of South Australia signed the Constitution. Next up was the Governor of Western Australia, who was then followed by the Administrator of the Northern Territory. The last person to sign the Constitution was of course, the President of the Republic of Australia, Christine Mills. After she scribbled her signature on the document, the Governors applauded, and more photos were taken.

9:49 AM.

Detective Sergeant Ethan Cooper and his former colleague, Max, finally arrived in Balmain, a suburb of Sydney. They pulled up a few hundred metres away from Grafton Lane, so they were not detected by the suspects. Ethan and Max got out of the car. As they did so, they withdrew their hand guns. Ethan Cooper had a Glock 19, a standard issue weapon of the Australian Federal Police. Max had a Beretta 92FS. Together, they sprinted down the footpath, in a flanked position. Max was behind Ethan and covered his back. They got to Grafton Lane and slowly made their way down it. Ethan looked up to see a drone hovering overhead. He pressed his finger on his earpiece radio. "This is Alpha One. We're fifty metres from the target. Any signs of hostiles?" asked Ethan. There was a delay in the response.

"Negative, Alpha One. No hostiles on site," said Felicity Meyers. She was the one who was controlling the drone. It was hovering over the address. Ethan and Max headed over to the address; it was a medium-sized storage unit split into two separate ones. As they got to the roller door, they were accompanied by six counterterrorist officers, wearing tactical gear and armed with assault rifles. One of them had a tactical shield to deflect gun fire. The officers came over to Ethan and Max. One of them snapped off the padlock with a pair of bolt cutters. Once that was done, Max and Ethan pulled up the roller door. It was a long rectangular shaped storage unit;

there was not much inside apart from several wooden boxes. However, in the centre of the unit, there was a large rectangular container. Its lid was off, and Ethan and Max slowly approached it. They shone their torches over it revealing the box was empty.

"Son of a bitch, it's empty," said Max.

"Are you sure this was the right address, Max?" asked Ethan.

"I'm positive, Ethan. This is where my contact said the weapons would be. Someone obviously got here first," he said. Ethan didn't say anything at first. He sighed and then got out his phone to dial a number.

"Mick Greer."

"It's me. We just searched the safe house. The weapons aren't here," said Ethan.

"Damn. Which means the terrorists are already in possession of the explosives," said Mick. Ethan didn't say anything after that.

"Detective Cooper!" one of the officers called out.

"Hold on." Ethan went over to where two officers were standing. They had their torches aimed at a picture on the wall. Ethan looked at it and he was shocked by what he saw. "My God...We've got a problem," he said.

"What is it, Ethan?"

"There's a photo on the wall in the storage unit...It's a photo of the Sydney Opera House," he said.

10:55 AM.

There were literally hundreds of people at the Sydney Opera House. They were all standing around the main steps where a staging area had been set up for the President of Australia to give her speech. Helicopters were flying overhead and captured breathtaking shots. A giant Australian flag was hung off the Sydney Harbour Bridge, of course, it was the new Australian republic flag, which was chosen by a separate referendum. Music was playing as people waited for the arrival of the President of Australia. A news reporter was standing near the entrance and was giving a live update on the event, stating that it was an overwhelming experience. Just then, the black Range Rover Vogue arrived on time. It was carrying the President of Australia, Christine Mills. People were screaming with excitement as they waved their own flags. A body-guard opened the rear door. Seconds later, Christine Mills emerged. The crowd erupted as she started waving at everyone.

She had a big smile on her face and began walked towards the stage. Of course, the crowds were blocked off by security fences, but that didn't stop Christine from mixing with her supporters. She shook hands with dozens of people, the whole time she walked towards the stage. After about five minutes of shaking hands, and getting photos taken, she finally made her way up to the centre stage.

She was then greeted by the Premier of New South Wales. "Ladies and gentlemen...I'd like to welcome to the stage, the first President of the Republic of Australia, our very own Australian head of state...Christine Mills!" said the Premier.

The crowds erupted with applause and continued shouting and whistling. Christine shook hands with the Premier, and she gave him a kiss on the cheek. She stepped up to the podium and stood there for a few moments as the crowd continued to go wild. She could barely get a word in. At last, they all started to settle down.

"Fellow Australians!" she said. Again, the crowd cheered and whistled. "Thank you all for coming out here on such a beautiful day," she began. "I can't begin to tell you how proud and honoured I am to be here today," she added. Joe Parsons was standing to the left of the stage and watched on as Christine spoke. "I was humbled, and certainly proud to be offered the opportunity to serve you, the Australian people, as your first head of state," she said. "I couldn't believe it when I heard the referendum to become a republic was a complete success...I was especially proud and privileged to give this speech on this day, January 26th, marking the anniversary of the 1788 arrival of the First Fleet of British ships at Port Jackson, and the raising of the flag of Great Britain at Sydney Cove." The crowd was captivated by the President's speech. "I would like to take this opportunity to show how grateful I am to be the first President of Australia...To be the first citizen to hold the highest office in all the land, and to be witness to the birth of a new era in history!" she shouted. More cheers and whistles were made. Joe knew that Christine was wrapping up her speech. As he stood there listening, Joe felt his phone vibrating. He quickly took it out to answer the incoming call.

"Joe Parsons!" he shouted, holding one finger against his ear. It was quite loud trying to hear who was on the other end.

"Mr. Parsons, this is Detective Chief Inspector Mick Greer, Serious Crimes Unit," said Mick.

"What's going on, Mick?"

"I'm calling to alert you to a situation. We've just found evidence that suggests the Opera House is the target for a terrorist attack," he said. Joe's eyes widened.

"Say that again, Mr. Greer?"

"I said, we found evidence the Opera House is the target for a terrorist attack…We believe terrorists managed to plant an explosive device inside the Opera House. We've got tactical police en-route to search the premises, but you need to evacuate the President, now," said Mick.

"Mr. Greer, the President is on stage giving her speech, I can't just drag her off," he said.

"Sir, a bomb is about to go off. Hundreds of lives are at stake. You need to get her out of there, now!" he shouted. Joe stood there, and hesitated. He then looked back at Christine, who was standing there smiling and waving.

"How long do we have?" asked Joe.

"It could go off any second, Mr. Parsons. You need to act, right now. Get her out of there!" Joe hung up the phone. Joe paused for a moment and then quickly went into action. He looked around for the nearest bodyguard. He spotted one standing near the stage, scanning the crowd, and on alert. Joe came over to him and whispered in the body-guard's ear. He immediately got on his radio to alert all other body-guards. At that, he got up onto the stage, and approached Christine. He leaned close to her ear. Then her eyes widened as she was told the shocking news. People in the crowd were starting to get confused as more body-guards dressed in black suits got up onto the stage and surrounded the President.

As they started moving her away, disrupting her speech, there was a sudden massive explosion. The explosion erupted through the centre of the Opera House and burst outwards like a volcano. Large chunks of the Opera House splashed into the water. Dozens of people were screaming and shouting in fear as more rubble landed near the staging area. A thick plume of smoke billowed from the large crater that appeared where the Opera House once was. The giant shell-shaped structures collapsed, and glass shattered everywhere. It was the most horrifying event to ever take place on Australian soil. A massive bomb exploded in the centre of the Sydney Opera House.

Dozens if not hundreds of people were screaming out in fear as large chunks of rubble rained down on the crowd of people. The Opera House was on fire, and it had exploded like a volcano had just erupted. A thick plume of black smoke rose into the air and there was nothing but silence. Within minutes of the bombing, police vehicles were on the scene, and helicopters were hovering overhead. On the harbour, the

AFP's water police were monitoring the situation and providing security. The event was being broadcasted on live TV across the entire nation. The air around the Opera House was thick and clogged by smoke and dust. The stage where the President of Australia, Christine Mills, was giving her speech had collapsed as a result of tons of concrete falling down on top of it. Christine was lying under a pile of rubble. She was unconscious, and barely moving. Rescue personnel managed to find her, and immediately started pulling away chunks of rock. It took a good five minutes before they got to the President. By that time, she'd just started coming to and she was very docile. "Ma'am, can you hear me?" said one of the paramedics, as they helped her to her feet. Her ears were ringing from the explosion. The rescue workers gently took hold of her, and carefully escorted her away from the site. The whole time she stepped, she could just see people trapped and crying out for help. Christine was taken to one of her backup vehicles that was parked a few hundred metres away. Her remaining security teams helped her into the back of the car, and within seconds, the car sped off. In the back, Christine looked over her shoulder, and she could see the Opera House in ruins.

Christine Mills was the President of Australia. She had been President for the past fourteen months, and she was still coming to terms with the idea; Christine's responsibility as the head of state of Australia was purely a ceremonial figurehead. Her position as head of state does not actively control policy in any aspect of the executive government. However, she does have some discretionary powers, such as the power to veto legislation. During the lead up to the republican referendum, there was much debate as to how to select a president. One side of the government were going with the idea of a directly elected president, meaning that the

Australian people would be voting for one single candidate to become president. Another idea was to suggest that the president be selected by directly elected by the parliament. This was ultimately the preferred choice and would be how the nation selects its president.

It had been over a year since the catastrophic bomb attack at the Sydney Opera House. Hundreds of people were killed, including the Premier of New South Wales. Although it had been twelve months since the explosion, the Opera House was still undergoing construction, as there was extensive damage to the building. Even though it had been a long time since the attack, Christine managed to find the courage to return to Sydney. Christine was at the Admiralty House, the official residence of the President of Australia. She was staying there with her husband, John Taylor, and they'd been there for the past couple of days in the lead up to the state funeral. However, today was a non-government working day. The entire country was in a state of shock and the nation was mourning the sudden death of the Prime Minister of Australia, Harold Samson. A state funeral was arranged for the Prime Minister and the memorial was to be held at St. Mary's Cathedral. Thousands of people were attending the state funeral, as was the current Prime Minister and the Premier of New South Wales. As part of her duties as the nation's first President, Christine was to give a eulogy to reflect on his service to the nation.

Christine had been awake since the early hours of the morning, thinking about the service. She was with her husband, John in the residence' main living room. The TV was on and it was showing a news report on the upcoming state funeral. There was a lot of arrangements to be made for this funeral, and security was to be tightened. They'd been watching the news for the past half an hour or so and were quite distraught by it all. Just then, there was a knock at the door. It was Joseph Parsons, Christine's Official Secretary. John Taylor got up and went to the door to let him in. Joe was dressed up in a black suit and tie and he too was feeling a bit overwhelmed by it all. "Morning, Mr. Taylor," said Joe, as he came in the door.

"Hey Joe, thanks for coming. Can I get you a coffee? Tea?" he asked.

"Coffee, thanks John…How is she?"

"She's a bit shaken up by it all."

"As is the rest of the country," said Joe.

"Where's Luke?"

"Ah, he's staying with his partner's family today. He didn't want anything to do with the service," said John. Luke was their twenty-year-old son.

"That's fair enough…Two sugars thanks John," said Joe. He started walking down the corridor and wandered into the lounge room where he saw Christine sitting there. She smiled as he came in. "Morning, Your Excellency," he said, closing the door. Christine looked up.

"Morning, Joe. Thanks for coming," she said, and Joe nodded.

"How are you coping?" She rolled her eyes.

"Oh, I think I'm okay. Just a bit of a shock that's all. Still can't believe the Prime Minister passed away," she replied. Joe fell silent after that and looked over at the TV. Right now, the report was going over the tragic events that happened that day.

"I just received word from Parliament House. The PM just left Canberra. He'll be here within the next hour," he said, and Christine nodded.

"Good. Is everything ready for the service?"

"Yes, I believe so. Are you still giving a eulogy?" he asked.

"Of course, Joe. Harold Samson was this nation's Prime Minister. He was well respected, and many people supported him. This is the best way to honour him," she said. The room fell silent after that, and Joe nodded.

"Okay, I'll run through the eulogy one last time," he said.

"Thanks Joe."

Mick Greer lived in the suburb of Pyrmont, Sydney. He owned a three-bedroom house, though he lived on his own. He did have a family; however, he'd just recently been through a divorce and his wife moved to Perth with their two children. It was just on eight o'clock in the morning. Mick was in the kitchen and making himself a cup of coffee. Today was a busy day for Mick. The AFP was providing security for the upcoming memorial service. As Mick stood there sipping his coffee, his Smartphone started ringing. "Mick Greer," he answered.

"Sir, it's Felicity Meyers. We've got a situation."

"What's going on Felicity?"

"ASIO raised the alert level. They believe there's a possibility of a terrorist attack," she said. There was a sudden pause. Mick stared at the TV for a second.

"Alright. Red flash the team and get them all in. I'll be there in ten minutes," said Mick, and hung up. He finished his coffee and put on his coat to leave for work.

Bondi Beach was empty. Samuel Hunter was a physical man of twenty-nine. He'd always been athletic and a bit of a jock during high school. Every morning, Sam went running along the beach to keep fit. He was obsessed with his health and fitness, and probably spent more time at the gym than at home. Though, since taking his new job, he barely had the time to hit the weights, so he went running as a substitute. He was a detective and had recently joined the Australian Federal Police; he signed up to the Serious Crimes Unit, and he was a detective constable. Today was his first official day on the job and he was quite excited. After running for about an hour, he jogged back to his house in Bondi Junction. Sam lived in a two-bedroom town house; it was one of those upmarket houses with a contemporary design and modern décor. It didn't have much of a backyard, but it did have a magnificent view of the beach. Sam loved it here, and he was already making friends with the neighbours. Of course, he didn't live alone. He was engaged to a beautiful woman named Rachel Parker. Rachel was a Registered Nurse and worked at the Royal Prince Alfred Hospital in the city. They planned on getting married in a few months, and they were busy trying to organise the wedding. Their jobs didn't make it any easier for them as finding the time to get stuff done was next to impossible.

Sam pushed through the front gate and went inside his brand-new house. They'd only just bought it and still unpacking some stuff. Sam came in through the front door. Exhausted from his run, he wandered into the kitchen. The TV was on in the lounge room, and it was displaying a news report about the upcoming state funeral for the Prime Minister of Australia, Harold Samson. As he came in, Rachel was there getting ready for work. "Morning," she said, as she tied up her blonde hair.

"Morning…Heading to work?" he asked.

"Yeah, someone called in sick, so I have to go in and cover. I had to reschedule the cake sampling again," she said, with frustration.

"I was so looking forward to eating cake," Sam said, with a chuckle. He grabbed an apple from the fruit bowl and bit into it.

"It's not funny, Sam. We're two months away from the wedding. Things still need to be done, the invitations still need to be posted, and you still need to arrange time off work," she said.

"Hey, hey…It's going to be okay." Rachel let out a sigh. "Come here." He took hold of her and they embraced.

"I love you, you know that?"

"Yes, I know."

"And we will get married in two months," he said. Rachel buried her head into Sam's chest, and he kissed her on the head. Just then, the phone started ringing. "Ugh, sorry." He reached over and picked it up. "Hello?"

"Hey Sam, it's Diane."

"Oh, hey Dee. What's up?"

"The boss wants us all in today. It's because of the memorial service." Sam closed his eyes.

"Yeah, alright. I understand. I'll be there in twenty," he said.

"Thanks Sam." Sam hung up and looked back at his frustrated fiancé.

"I have to go into work too," he said. They both just looked at each other.

John Taylor and Christine Mills had been together for the past twenty odd years and loved each other very much. When they got married, Christine kept her maiden name as she didn't want to change it. Since Christine entered a life of politics, John had supported his wife every single day and wanted her to be successful. After being appointed the first President of Australia, John became a well-liked man. However, he had been suffering from depression, as well as grief. Eighteen months ago, he and Christine lost their daughter, Amanda. She allegedly committed suicide, but it was never proven. For six months, her death had been in the papers and it was a daily hot topic for news channels. After a thorough investigation by the Australian Federal Police, it was revealed that she did in fact commit suicide, and the case was closed. But of course, John refused to believe it. He was convinced that her death was not a suicide, and that she'd been murdered by someone. He spent the last couple of months attempting to find out the truth about her death.

After Christine left for the office, John found himself standing by the window gazing out into oblivion. He stood there sipping his cup of coffee and dwelled on Amanda's death. Attending a memorial service bought back some unwanted memories of Amanda's funeral. It wasn't a big service, just a small gathering of the family. But he just never got over it, as any parent wouldn't forget their child's parting. At times, he'd often felt alone; but he wasn't alone. He had a private body-guard, Mitch Clark. Several months ago, he was hired to protect John, as he'd received multiple death threats. This morning, he was having a private session with his psychologist, Rebecca Scott. She'd been treating him for his depression and grief and helped him a lot in the past twelve months. He was especially grateful for her being here today, as the service brought up so many memories. "So, how are you feeling today, John? I know it's a bit of an open-ended question, but I want to help you through this," said Rebecca, as she sat there on the couch. John didn't reply straight away. He already had tears in his eyes, as he thought about Amanda.

"You know it's hard...There's not a single day that goes by that I don't think about her," he said.

"I'd be very worried if you weren't John. Are you still taking the medication?" she asked, and John nodded.

"Yes. It helps ease the pain and to get me through the day," he replied. "It's just that every time I read the paper, or watch the news, there's always something on there about Amanda's suicide...I still don't believe she killed herself," he said.

"You still believe she was murdered by someone?"

"Of course, she was Rebecca. My daughter was not suicidal...She was happy, she was engaged to be married...Why would she commit suicide?" Rebecca didn't reply straight away.

"Sometimes we just don't fully understand how people are feeling. She was probably upset about something and she may have felt trapped by it," said Rebecca.

"I just wished she'd come to us for help…It's not like we weren't speaking to one another," he said. She didn't reply straight away. Just then, John's body-guard, Mitch Clark, came in.

"Excuse me, Sir. You have a phone call," he said, holding a phone.

"Excuse me, we're in the middle of a session here," said Rebecca, standing up.

"It's okay, Rebecca…I could use a break anyway," said John. He came over to Mitch who stood by the door. "Who is it?" he asked. Mitch leaned forward.

"It's Rick Wilson, Sir," he said. John's eyes widened, as he knew who it was. He took the phone and walked over to the corner. "Hello Rick. It's John." Rick was a private detective, and he was helping John with a case.

"John, I'm glad I caught you…I have some additional information regarding your daughter's suicide," he began.

"Don't you mean her 'alleged suicide'?" he said.

"Right, sorry. Anyway, I need to meet you to discuss this evidence. Are you free?" John sighed and thought for a moment. He checked his watch.

"Sure, I can meet you in half an hour?"

"Sounds good. I'll meet you at Hyde Park, the water fountain," he said, and then hung up. John stood there and was curious about what Rick had to say about Amanda's death.

The Serious Crimes Unit operated on a twenty-four-hour schedule. The SCU was a non-departmental public body of the Government of Australia. The SCU was a national law enforcement agency with Australian Government sponsorship, established as a body corporate under Section 1 of the Serious Organised Crime and Police Act 2005. It operated within Australia and collaborated with the Australian Federal Police. Its headquarters was in a large warehouse style building with brick walls and metal support beams. The agency was split into several levels with the main operations command centre being on the first level. This was where all the action took place and the point of entry for its personnel. The agency was funded through the federal government and was equipped with all the latest technology.

It was a typical morning at the SCU and since there was a major event taking place in Sydney, many of the agency's personnel were hard at work. Since it was the first line of defence, the SCU had been put in charge of security for the state funeral. Felicity was sitting at her desk, a large rounded shaped desk which was positioned in the middle of the operations centre; this enabled her to keep an eye on her team of analysts. She had three large twenty-seven-inch monitors along with all the typical office equipment. As she flicked through some intelligence reports, a hand tapped her on the shoulder. She literally jumped out of her skin and her heart sank. "Jesus, you scared the shit out of me!" she cursed, as she turned around.

"Sorry Felicity, didn't mean to scare you," said Detective Sergeant Diane Faulkner. Diane was a woman in her late thirties, and quite a successful woman at that. Diane was one of those women who thought she was better than anyone else and liked to know everything before anyone else. She never had any patience for drama which was a common occurrence around the office. But there was one thing she liked; it was Felicity Meyers. She respected her in many ways, mostly because she trusted Felicity and vice versa. She was someone who she could tell anything and confide in. Often, Felicity would tell her things the moment she received them, such as intelligence updates.

"Don't do that to me again," she replied, still trying to collect her breath.

"I come bearing gifts." Diane placed a take away coffee on her desk and a muffin. Felicity liked the blue berry muffins from the cafe just down the road.

"You're an absolute life saver," she said, and took a bite of the muffin.

"So, what's the big emergency?" she asked, changing the subject.

"Mr. Greer asked me to bring everyone in. ASIO raised the terrorist alert level," said Felicity. Diane rolled her eyes in anguish.

"Ugh, today is going to be a long day...Is everyone else in?"

"Ah, Greer's on his way, the Boss lady is in her office," said Felicity. Diane walked over to her desk which was opposite Felicity's station and sat down to get to work. The elevator doors opened. Detective Chief Inspector Mick Greer stepped out. He was on the phone talking to the Assistant Commissioner while also holding his morning coffee and carrying his briefcase. "Yes, I'll update you every half an hour. Thank you." Then he hung up, frustrated. "Morning Felicity. Updates?" he asked.

"Morning to you too Boss…Nothing out of the ordinary. Just keeping an eye on the area. First security sweep has been completed. No signs of any explosive devices," she said.

"Well let's hope it stays that way. Is everyone in?" "Just about. Diane just got here," she said.

"Alright. Let me know as soon as the others get here." She nodded.

"Oh, by the way, the Boss lady is in her office," she said. Mick paused for a moment. He turned his head and saw Anna Mackenzie standing in her office.

"Great. This day just keeps on getting better and better," he said, with sarcasm. Felicity just smiled. "I'll be in my office," he said, and made his way across the floor. He started climbing the stairs to the upper levels. He approached his office door and hesitated for a moment, then went in. She was currently talking on the phone, probably to the Commissioner. He decided to let himself in, despite knowing the risks. Anna Mackenzie was the Superintendent and the head of the SCU. She reported directly to the Commissioner.

"Yes, Sir. That's affirmative. I'll keep you informed of any progress," she said, and then hung up. "Morning, Greer. Nice of you to grace the office with your presence," she said.

"Well, and a good morning to you," he replied, sarcastically. Anna just gave him an odd look.

"Mick, you know what kind of day it's going to be. I could do without the sarcasm."

"Alright, sorry…Who was that?"

"The Commissioner. He informed me the Prime Minister is on his way. So, we don't have a lot of time before the service starts," she said.

"What's the latest?"

"Final security sweeps have been completed. No sign of any explosive devices," said Mick.

"Good. The Commissioner is concerned about the possibility of a terrorist attack. He's recommending postponing it."

"Any idea on what sort of threat?"

"No. But with the PM and the President in attendance, any threat is considered serious. We need to make sure nothing happens."

"And nothing will. We've got the entire area secure," he assured her. But Anna didn't look convinced.

"Yes well, regardless of that, we need to deal with this threat. I want you and your people on top of this situation."

John Taylor was still thinking about the conversation he had with Rick Wilson. He couldn't believe what he'd said on the phone about Amanda's fiancé and that he had evidence indicating he had knowledge of Amanda's death. John sat in the back seat of his car and stared out the window, constantly thinking about Amanda. It seemed like they'd been driving forever, but in fact, it'd only been about ten minutes; they'd finally arrived at Sydney's Hyde Park. John got out of the car and made his way through the cast iron gates that made up the park's entrance. He was escorted by his body-guard Mitch Clark, and they approached the water fountain. There was a park bench next to it and he spotted a man sitting there reading the newspaper. He identified who it was straight away and turned back to Mitch. He indicated that he didn't want him to follow any further. Mitch respected his command and stood within proximity. John's heart was racing the whole time he walked over to the park bench. He sat down an arm's length away from Rick who wore a brown jacket, as the weather was quite cool. It was coming into autumn and most of the trees were losing their leaves. "So, what's this evidence you have?" asked John. Rick Wilson continued reading his paper.

"It doesn't look good John...I found bank statements from your daughter's fiancé`. It shows he received a sum of two hundred thousand dollars two days after her suicide," said Rick. John's eyes widened.

"Are you saying my daughter's fiancé` had something to do with her death?"

"It's possible. But it doesn't look good either way. Are you still in contact with him?"

"No. I haven't spoken with Andy since the funeral," said John. "I can't believe he's involved."

"I don't know if he is involved or not. But one way or another, he should be treated as suspicious," said Rick. "Here's a copy of his recent bank statements. You want me to question him?" John shook his head.

"No, it's okay. Andy won't talk to a private investigator. I'll confront him myself," said John. He paused for a moment as someone walked past. "Thanks Rick, I owe you big time," he added. He reached over, and they shook hands.

It was just after nine o'clock in the morning. Ethan Cooper found himself passed out on the couch. He had been through a lot over the past twelve months. Ethan Cooper decided to retire from the Serious Crimes Unit, as he spent six months hunting down the people responsible for the terrorist attack on the Sydney Opera House. He wanted to make them pay for what they did and the amount of lives they destroyed. After finding the person who ordered the bombing, he went a bit too far during the questioning of the suspect; to a point where the suspect ended up in hospital. His retirement wasn't exactly voluntary, he was put on a temporary leave of absence until his case was put through a hearing. He chose instead to resign to not be a disgrace to the Serious Crimes Unit.

For a long time, Ethan Cooper struggled with the idea of being an unemployed bum. However, it wasn't like he was living on the streets or anything; it was the exact opposite. It was thanks to the AFP's retirement fund that he was able to keep living in his fancy contemporary townhouse in Sydney's Newtown. It was an expensive apartment on Camden Street, with easy access to everything, not that he went anywhere most days, except for the local pub, which he could be found there most nights. He would usually end up going to the pub around seven o'clock at night and would get himself to bed around three in the morning with a massive migraine. He certainly did miss working at the SCU. He missed the thrill of it, but he knew it was the right decision to leave when he did. For a month or so, Ethan kept receiving calls from them, asking him, no, begging him to come back to work, but he just refused. Ethan hated this time of year, as it always brought back horrible memories. He still got flash backs from that day, and he could hear the massive explosion that took place at the Sydney Opera House. He could also hear the screams of innocent people as they fled the scene. Ethan usually drowned the sound with booze. The next morning, he woke up suddenly to the sound of the TV. He wasn't quite sure why it was on; he must've left it on all night. It was a news report on the upcoming state funeral. He got up to make himself a coffee and checked his phone to see if there were any missed calls or messages; there were none. As he stood there sipping his morning coffee, he glanced over at a photo of himself and his wife, Susan. He thought back to the day when she passed away.

2 Years Ago.

There were no words to describe how Ethan Cooper was feeling. Especially since he did just bury his wife, Susan Cooper. He had just been to her funeral service; she recently passed away due to breast cancer, which she discovered too late, and it consumed her body. Ethan sat in the front seat of his car, a black Holden Commodore SV6. He sat there dazing into oblivion. All he could think about was Susan lying on her death bed and seeing how much she was suffering. It was one of the worst days of his life and he could only imagine how his daughter was feeling. She was staying with her Grandparents for a while, so she could have someone to keep her company. Ethan wasn't in the best frame of mind to be looking after his daughter.

Ethan was wearing his Army uniform – Ethan Cooper was a First Lieutenant in the Australian Army's Special Air Service Regiment, a special operations unit that deal with high-profile operations. He was on an operation when he found out that Susan was sick. After that, he immediately requested a temporary discharge from the Army, so he could be with his family. The Army accepted, and he immediately flew back to Sydney.

Ethan hated funerals. He hated going to them ever since his Grandfather died several years before hand. He just had no idea what he was feeling right now. He felt disconnected from everyone, despite all his family being there, his mother, his dad, and his twin sister were there to support him and his daughter, but he just didn't want to face them right now. He wanted to be alone, and drown his sorrows with a large drink, preferably alcoholic. Despite feeling like shit, Ethan drove back to his local town and went into the pub where he ordered a double shot of Whiskey. He took a sip of it and looked up at the TV above the bar. It was a news report stating that the government were planning to conduct a referendum. It was to see whether or not the general public were in favour of Australia becoming a republic; for weeks, it had sparked much debate and discussion. Many people were opposed the idea, yet far more were liking the decision. Of course, Ethan only just recently found out about the proposed referendum, since he was in Afghanistan at the time. Ethan ordered another drink, another shot of Whiskey. "I thought I'd fine you here," a familiar voice spoke from behind him. Ethan put the glass down and swung around to see who it was. He was certainly shocked to see that it was in fact Mick Greer, an old friend of his. Ethan and Mick had known each other for quite some time and had become good friends.

"Hey Mick. I never expected to see you here," said Ethan, and went back to his drink.

"Well, I knew this is where you'd be after the funeral…I'm terribly sorry for the loss, Ethan. I can't begin to imagine what you're feeling," said Mick, as he sat on the stool next to Ethan. Ethan scoffed and downed his drink.

"I feel like shit," he said. Mick slowly nodded.

"I can understand that…I see you're shipping out soon?" asked Mick, looking at his uniform.

"Yeah, I got new orders from command. The unit is being called back," said Ethan.

"I see…Well that's a shame, because I've got a job offer for you," said Mick. He had a folder in his hand and placed it next to Ethan. Of course, he didn't really care to begin with.

"What kind of job?" he asked.

"There's a new unit being setup. It's an entity of the AFP...The Serious Crimes Unit," he said. "I've been put in charge of this task force, as Detective Chief Inspector."

"Well, I believe a congratulations is in order," said Ethan, raising his third glass of Whiskey into the air.

"I was kind of hoping you'd be interested in coming to work for me...At the Serious Crimes Unit," said Mick. Ethan nearly spat out his drink.

"You're kidding me?" But Mick just shook his head. "You want me to come work for you? As what?"

"How does Detective Sergeant Ethan Cooper sound to you?" he asked. Ethan didn't reply straight away. "Of course, you'll have to go through the proper detective training with the AFP, but since you're already an SASR officer, I'm sure it wouldn't be too much different," said Mick.

"I can't just say yes. I've got my orders, I'm shipping out tomorrow morning," said Ethan.

"Yes, about that...I've spoken with your commanding officer. He and I both agree that you will need to spend some time to deal with your wife's passing. I told him I was interested in pursuing you with a job offer, and he accepted my proposal."

"Is that so?" asked Ethan.

"Like I said, the jobs yours if you want it," said Mick. He finished his drink and got off the stool. "You're one of a kind, Ethan. You're what this unit needs. This country is being faced with some serious challenges in the near future, and lots of people are going to be against those changes. We need people like you on our side," said Mick. "Just think it over…You know how to reach me." Mick tapped Ethan on the shoulder a couple of times. "Take care of yourself buddy."

Just then, his day dream was disrupted. He looked up to the sound of banging on his apartment door. He was surprised at the knocking and was confused by who it was. He wasn't expecting anyone today, certainly not at this time of the morning. He waited for a moment, to see if it'd stopped. But then, there was more banging. So, he got up and went to the door. He pulled the door slightly ajar to see who it was. "Who is it?" he asked, standing there with his gun ready.

"It's me, Ethan. Open up," said a familiar voice.

"Alex?"

"Yeah. Let me in, please. We need to talk," he said. Ethan just rolled his eyes.

"This better be important Alex." Then he opened the door and Alex wandered in. He immediately shut the door and locked it.

"I'm in trouble," he said, as he gasped for air. Alex Morgan was another member of Ethan's squad in the SASR. He and Ethan had been friends for quite some time.

"What the hell are you doing here?"

"You need to call the SCU. I have Intel on a terrorist threat," he said. Ethan looked at him, sharply.

"Damn it, Alex. I'm retired!" he said.

"This is important, Ethan…I went to meet a contact of mine. He said he managed to get some Intel behind a terror plot. It's supposed to be going down today," said Alex.

"Does this have something to do with the state funeral?" he asked.

"Yeah, it's connected. I found out that these people are planning a major attack today."

"Jesus. What kind of attack?"

"I don't know, but looks like the Universal Adversary Group is behind it," said Alex.

The Universal Adversary Group, or UAG for short, was a criminal organization who were very anti-government, and hated politics. Their goal was to destabilize the government by carrying out acts of politically motivated violence and chaos. They operated in a similar way to the Irish Republican Army.

"Son of a bitch…How are they carrying it out?" Alex didn't say anything straight away.

"My contact told me that it has something to do with explosives," he said. Ethan's eyes widened. "How good is this Intel?"

"Very good. My contact was killed getting me the Intel. He managed to give me a thumb drive containing encrypted data about who's involved in this conspiracy," he explained. Ethan didn't know what to say about all of this and let out a sigh.

"You'd better not be screwing with me." Ethan went over to the coffee table. He picked up his mobile phone and started dialling a number. As he waited for the call to connect, he turned to the TV and saw the report on the memorial service.

"Operations Centre, how can I direct your call?"

"Yes, this is Ethan Cooper. I need to speak with Detective Chief Inspector Mick Greer, ASAP," he requested.

"One moment." The operator then transferred the call.

"Ethan? This is an unexpected surprise…How are you?" asked Mick, as he sat at his desk. He and Ethan were good friends, and he looked out for him as he went through the difficult grieving process.

"Mick, I'm fine. I don't have a lot of time. I've just had a visit from an old friend of mine. He says he's got Intel on an attack in Sydney."

"Bloody oath…What kind of attack?"

"I don't know. But he said the UAG is behind it…Mick, this is serious."

"Jesus…How good is this Intel?" asked Mick.

"Very. It's on an encrypted hard drive. We're going to need someone to decrypt it," said Ethan.

"Alright. I'll assign it to Felicity. How far away are you?"

"Okay, fine. We're less than ten minutes out," said Ethan.

"Okay good. Get here as soon as you can Ethan…And be careful," said Mick. "I will." Ethan hung up and looked back at Alex.

"So, what did they say?"

"Mick wants me to bring you in…I just hope this evidence you have is trustworthy," said Ethan.

"Trust me, Ethan. The SCU need to see what I have," said Alex. Ethan didn't say anything after that. They made their way to the front door. Ethan's car was parked on the side of the road and they headed down the footpath. As they were about to get into the car, a dark coloured van came speeding around the corner. Ethan looked up to see what the noise was. He saw the van come speeding towards them. As it got closer, it began to slow down. Its side door opened, and a masked man poked his head out. He held a semiautomatic machine gun and open-fired at Ethan and Alex. Alex grabbed onto Ethan and pulled him down behind Ethan's car. Bullets sprayed everywhere, smashing up the windows and denting the body of his car. It was all over within a matter of seconds. Then the van sped off and disappeared. Ethan's heart was racing as he took cover behind one of the wheels. He cautiously peered over the bonnet to see if it was safe. He could see the van speeding away and raced around the corner.

"Jesus. Who the hell was that?" said Ethan. But there was no response.

"Alex?" he looked over and saw Alex lying on the footpath, choking. He'd been shot in the neck and he was coughing up blood. "Fucking son of a bitch," he cursed. He went over to him and supported his friend. "Come on, Alex. Stay with me, damn it!" he said, as he pressed down on the gunshot wound. As he did so, he took out his phone to dial triple zero. "This is Ethan Cooper. I need an ambulance immediately!" he shouted.

John couldn't get over what his private detective told him. The fact that Amanda's fiancé` Andrew Shaw received a considerable sum of money two days after her suicide raised some concerning questions. He was going to get to the bottom of this no matter what. He was on his way over to Andrew's apartment, as he knew where he lived. His private body-guard, Mitch Clark, was a little bit concerned about what John was doing, and he was worried about him. "Are you sure this is a good idea, Sir?" he asked, as they drove. John looked at him.

"Of course, Mitch. If Rick found evidence suggesting my former son-in-law had something to do with my daughter's death, then I want to know about it," he said. Mitch didn't reply straight away and looked back at the road.

"I just think it's a mistake to confront him like this."

"Look, I respect you're thinking of my welfare. But for the last six months I've been told that my only daughter committed suicide from a drug overdose," he said. "There's one thing that is inconsistent...My daughter never took drugs." They pulled up to an intersection with a red light. There was a pause in the conversation. Just then, Mitch's phone rang.

"Mitch Clark," he answered. "One moment." Mitch looked over his shoulder and handed the phone to John who was staring out the window again. "Sir, it's the President." John quickly took the phone.

"Hi sweetheart."

"Hi...I just wanted to make sure you were okay. I knew you had a meeting with Rebecca today," she said. John smiled.

"Yes, it was fine. It was good to talk to someone about it." Christine smiled.

"That's good. I've been thinking about her all morning too," she said. There was a slight pause in the conversation. "Are you on your way to the service?" John paused, as he thought about what to say. "Ah, not yet no. I have an errand to run first," he said.

"Oh, I see…What sort of errand?" she asked. John rolled his eyes.

"Come on now, Christine. Does that really matter?"

"No, I was just curious. I'm just worried about you, John," she replied.

"Thank you, but you don't need to be. I'm fine…To be honest, I'm going to pay Andy a visit," he said.

"Andrew? What for?" she asked, curiously. John let out a sigh.

"A few months ago, I hired a private detective to look into Amanda's death…He found some pretty convincing evidence against Andy," said John.

"I don't believe this…You hired a God damn private detective?" she snapped.

"I had to, Christine. The AFP finished their investigation and all they found was that she killed herself from a drug overdose," said John, abruptly.

"John, I know you're still grieving, believe me, as am I. But what you're doing is borderline paranoia," said Christine.

"See, this is why I didn't want to tell you about this, Christine…Regardless, I'm doing this for my sake…We'll talk later."

"John, please. Talk to me," she said. But just then, John hung up the phone. The car had stopped.

Mitch Clark looked over his shoulder.

"We're here Sir," he said, and John nodded. He got out and made his way over to the front entrance to the apartment building. It was a town house with a contemporary design to it. John walked up the front steps and rang the doorbell. A few moments later, it opened, and to his surprise, Andrew Shaw stood there in the door way.

"Mr. Taylor, this is quite the surprise. What brings you here?" he asked. John just stared at him.

"I think you know why I'm here, Andy...We need to talk," he said.

"Sure, come on in." Andrew showed him in. They made their way down the wooden floorboard corridor and ended up in the kitchen. "Can I get you a cup of coffee?" he asked.

"No, thank you. I won't be staying long...I've come to ask you about Amanda's death," he began. Andrew stopped what he was doing and looked at him.

"What about it?"

"Two days after her death, you received a bank transfer of over two hundred thousand dollars...Where the bloody hell did you get it from?" John snapped.

"I have no idea what you're talking about, John. I didn't receive any such money," he said. John walked up to him with a stern look on his face.

"I know you're lying, Andy. Who gave you that money?" he demanded. Andy let out a sigh.

"Alright, fine...You want to know where I got that money from?" he said. "It was my inheritance, from my father," he said. John didn't know what to say to that. "My father passed away six months before Amanda...You know, and the inheritance has only just been processed," he replied. Again,

John remained silent. He was somewhat thrown off by all of this. "I realise it's been tough for you John, but I know what you're going through." The room fell silent after that.

"I'm sorry, Andy…I don't know what to say," he said.

"It's okay, John. I understand what you were doing, and I'd be doing the exact same thing," said Andy. They both just stood there, not saying anything.

Ethan arrived at the Alfred Hospital. The ambulance pulled up to the emergency bay and several paramedics climbed out. Alex was lying on the hospital bed with an oxygen mask over his mouth and he was in and out of consciousness. The medics quickly wheeled him into the main entrance and rushed him into the operating theatre. He followed them in, and as he walked, he took out his mobile phone to dial a number. "Mick Greer."

"Hey, it's me. There's been a delay."

"What's wrong, Ethan?" "Alex Morgan's been shot."

"Bloody hell. Who shot him?"

"I'm not sure. We were just leaving my place when we were attacked by an unmarked van. Any chance you could get someone to access any CCTV footage in that area?"

"Yeah, I'll put Felicity on to it. What about that evidence?"

"Alex gave me the hard drive. He said it's encrypted, so you'll need someone to look at it," said Ethan.

"Alright. I'll get Felicity working on the CCTV. Do you know how long it will be before you can talk to Morgan?"

"No. I'm about to talk to the doctors, then I'll head over to the agency," he said, and then hung up. Ethan stood there and began to feel kind of worried. Mick hung up the phone. He thought for a moment and then quickly headed out the door of his office. He walked over to Felicity's station. Everyone else was busy working away.

"Felicity. I need you to do something for me...Are there any CCTV cameras in the area where Ethan Cooper lives? He lives in Newtown." Felicity looked at him, puzzled.

"Ah, there might be. Let me just check," she said. She then typed at her computer. A few moments later, she brought up a window on her screen. "It looks like there's several."

"Okay, bring up footage from one of the cameras. Play the footage going back twenty minutes, please," said Mick. She continued to type at her computer. Then, within a matter of a few seconds, she brought up a digital playback of CCTV footage. They both watched it and it showed Ethan Cooper and Alex Morgan coming out from his house. It showed them walking to his car, and then suddenly a van came speeding towards them. Felicity gasped as she saw what happened next.

"My God...What happened?"

"Ethan's in a bit of trouble. He's bringing in a hard drive. It has Intel on a planned terrorist attack. He said it's been encrypted, so I'll need you to get onto that," said Mick.

"Okay, I'll run a decryption program," she added. Just then, Sam and Diane Faulkner came over to them.

"Hey Boss. Just letting you know I'm here," she said. Mick turned around.

"Good. There's a briefing in ten minutes...And this must be?"

"Detective Constable Sam Hunter."

"Right, of course. Sorry Sam, my minds all confused at the moment. We've got a lot going on right now...I appreciate you coming in today," he said, and Sam nodded. "How was the anti-terrorist training?"

"It was brilliant," he replied. Mick was surprised by his enthusiasm, as most of the seasoned officers who'd done that training course found it horrible and boring. "Detective Faulkner tells me you're a stellar recruit...Glad to have you on board," he said.

"Thank you, Sir." They shook hands.

"So, what's the emergency?" asked Diane, changing the subject.

"I'll explain in the briefing, but suffice it to say, the agency has increased its terror alert status. I received a call from Ethan Cooper. He was given an encrypted hard drive with Intel on the attack," said Mick.

"Jesus...Any idea what sort of attack?" said Diane, but Mick shook his head.

"Wait, who's Ethan Cooper?" asked Sam, looking confused.

"Ethan Cooper is ex-SASR. He's one of our best detectives...Felicity, why don't you take Sam over to his station and get him set up?" he asked, and Felicity nodded. She escorted Sam across the floor.

"Are you sure it's a good idea to bring Ethan into this? You know, considering what he's been through?" said Diane.

"I know. But the fact is, we need him today, Diane. Something big is going down, and we need his help," said Mick. "Prepare for the briefing." Diane didn't say anything after that and walked off to her station.

"Gentlemen, the meeting will now come to order." Fourteen men had gathered in the main board room. The board room was located on the top floor of the Birchall McClelland headquarters. The BMC building was located in Sydney, the flagship headquarters of the organisation and occupied two thirds of the Governor Phillip Tower in Sydney's financial district. The building stood an impressive two hundred and twenty-seven metres into the air and was one of the tallest buildings in the city. The board room was set up just like any ordinary executive office boardroom. In the centre was a large square shaped table with fifteen executive office chairs around it. Of course, one of them was at the front, reserved for the Chairman of the Board.

Ten of the men sat in padded office chairs around the conference table. The men represented various intelligence organizations and branches of the Australian defence department. Against one wall, four more men sat in folding chairs. These men represented four broad civilian industries, including coal mining, oil and natural gas, banking and finance, and aerospace and defence.

The group operated in secrecy, even from itself. No one in the room wore identifying markers of any kind. There were no name plates, no indications of rank, and no combat ribbons or medals in evidence. Indeed, there were no uniforms. The military men all wore dress shirts and slacks. Although most of the men knew one another to some degree, two of the men were strangers, and had affiliations that were unclear to the rest of the group.

A silver-haired four-star general, once a commander in the Army, stood at the head of the table. He rubbed an old, long-faded scar on his forehead. It was Karl Benedict, the Chief Executive Officer of Birchall McClelland. "You all know me," he said. "You know my role here. So, I'll get right to it. Events have moved forward quickly in the past twenty-four hours, faster than we could have anticipated. I realise that past events were supposed to show this country that we mean business…However, it would seem that it's not the case," said Karl Benedict. "I know that you're all against the idea of this country becoming a republic, and I know that you're all hating that this country has a woman as its head of state," said Karl. "I'd like to assure you all here today, that I, Karl Benedict, the Chief Executive Officer of Birchall McClelland, has sworn an oath to protect the Australian people from this disaster," said Karl. There was an eerie silence in the room as he looked around at all the members.

A hand at the table was raised. Karl recognized a man much older than himself, a former Navy admiral. There was an iconic photograph from the event, which had never been declassified, but which the general had seen. It showed the admiral at nineteen years of age, shirtless in a muddy trench, his eyes wild, his face and upper body painted dark red with the blood of dead communists. "Yes?" Mr. Benedict asked.

"Just what exactly are you proposing, Mr. Benedict?" asked one of the members. Karl didn't reply straight away, and he grinned.

"I appreciate your curiosity. What I am proposing, will change this country."

"Do you anticipate that it will cause any problems?" said another member.

Karl picked up the paper in front of him and began to carefully shred it into long narrow strips.

"We don't anticipate," he said, "any problems at all." There was silence across the room. "Now, moving on…According to my notes, some of you have expressed concerns with this operation," he said. "Let me assure you, that this operation will help ensure the safety and the future of the Australian government…I realize that it is a drastic measure, to allow terrorists to carry out attacks on Australian soil, but we need to show this government is weak, and the Australian people deserve better," he said. "I believe that a regime change in this country will make it stronger, and we can achieve those goals…Let's stand together, and let's make Australia great again!" the others around the table started clapping.

Christine Mills sat at her desk. She was going over her eulogy for the service and catching up on the morning news. There was a news report on Prime Minister Stephen Brown's parliamentary address earlier regarding the rising threat of terrorism in Australia and in Sydney. He was calling for extraordinary measures to be introduced to combat terror threats. There was also an update on the upcoming state funeral in Sydney. As she sat there, the door opened and her executive assistant, Brian Stedman stepped in. "Your

Excellency, your husband is here," he said, and she nodded. A few moments later, John Taylor came in. Christine muted the TV and put her cup of coffee down.

"Hi," he said, as he closed the door.

"Hi...I wasn't expecting to see you," said Christine. John didn't say anything at first.

"I came to apologize for my behaviour earlier...I didn't mean to snap at you like that," he said. Christine smiled.

"It's fine, apology accepted. I just wished you'd come to me first about this," said Christine.

"What made you hire a private detective?"

"Because I still believe our daughter did not commit suicide. She was murdered, Christine. This is the only way I'm going to prove it," he replied. Christine closed her eyes.

"Sweetheart, the AFP carried out a full investigation. They proved it was suicide."

"I can't believe you would think that our daughter ever had suicidal tendencies," said John. The room fell silent after that.

"So, what did Andy have to say?" asked Christine, changing the subject.

"Not a whole lot...He received over two hundred thousand dollars two days after Amanda's death. I thought he knew something about it and assumed he was paid to keep quiet about it."

"And was he?" John slowly shook his head.

"No...Turns out the money was from his father's inheritance," said John. Christine shook her head in disbelief.

"I hope you learnt your lesson, John...Now, I have a memorial service to prepare for, and I need your support. The PM is on his way and I can't be distracted by this," she said. John didn't say anything after that. Just then, there was another knock at the door.

"Come in!" it opened, and Joe Parsons entered.

"Oh, sorry I didn't mean to interrupt."

"It's fine, Joe. What is it?" she asked.

"The PM just landed. He's on his way to St Mary's Cathedral," he said, and Christine nodded.

"Thanks Joe. I'm almost ready to leave." He closed the door. Christine stood up and started putting on her coat. "Please stop worrying about this, John. I miss Amanda just as much as you. But unfortunately, I have memorial service to attend," she said. Of course, John didn't respond. She kissed him on the cheek and then headed to the door. Joe was waiting for her.

"Everything alright, Ma'am?" he asked, as they started making their way down the corridor.

"Oh, yes Joe. Just stuff between John and I," she said. They came down to the main foyer of the residence. Outside, Christine's escort vehicle was waiting for her; she climbed into the back of the black Range Rover Sports and it slowly drove off.

John Taylor was still in Christine's office. He couldn't get over Christine's response to his claims that Andy knew something about Amanda's death. As he stood there in dismay, his mobile phone started ringing. "John Taylor," he answered.

"Hey John, it's me. Andy," he said.

"Oh, hi Andy. What can I do for you?" he asked.

"I wanted to apologize for the way I acted earlier," he said.

"No, don't be silly Andy. It's me who should be apologizing. I was out of line accusing you of something you didn't do," he said.

"The truth is…You were right." John's eyes widened.

"Right about what, Andy?"

"About the two hundred thousand dollars…It wasn't an inheritance. I was paid off because I know what happened to Amanda," he explained. John couldn't believe.

"I'm sorry, I don't understand. You're saying I was right about her being murdered?"

"Yes…Someone killed her because she uncovered a conspiracy."

"My God…What kind of conspiracy?"

"I can't discuss it over the phone. I think I'm being watched…Can we meet somewhere?" John checked his watch.

"Ah, sure. Where?"

"Meet me at the Sydney Tower restaurant in fifteen minutes?" he asked.

"Yeah, sure I'll be there...And Andy, thank you," he finished, and hung up.

Since he was forced to resign from the Serious Crimes Unit, Ethan Cooper never expected to be getting back to work so soon. But he didn't really have much of a choice, since he was forced into this situation. Though he couldn't just ignore it as there were innocent lives at stake, and it was his mission to protect Australian lives. He pulled into the SCU's underground parking garage. He was cleared through security and found himself a parking spot. He turned the ignition off but instead of getting out, he just sat there for a moment. He was still in shock about what had happened at his place. The fact that someone just tried to kill him, and his best friend was overwhelming to say the least. Ethan got out of his car and he was escorted into the building by a security officer. After boarding the elevator, they arrived at the main operations centre. The place was busy as usual. The security guard led him over to Mick. "Chief Inspector, I assume this one is for you?" he asked. Mick turned around and nodded.

"Yes, thank you officer," said Mick. "Ethan, good to see you again." The two embraced.

"You too," he said.

"Look, I realize this must be awkward for you, since you were forced to resign," said Mick.

"It's fine, Boss. I'm not going to make a scene."

"Right, well, I've spoken with Mackenzie. She's authorized your temporary reinstatement," he said.

"How'd you manage to pull that off?"

"We're dealing with a serious situation, Ethan. After the Independence Day terrorist attack, no threat is being taken lightly," he replied. "Also, you're one of our best." They both fell silent after that. "So…How's Alex?"

"He's lost a lot of blood, he's been put into an induced coma," said Ethan. "Hopefully he pulls through."

"I hope so too, because the memorial service is in less than an hour," said Mick. Ethan slowly nodded. Just then, Diane and Sam came over. "Anyway, welcome back to the team," he said. "By the way, Ethan Cooper, this is Detective Constable Samuel Hunter. Detective Hunter just joined us from the academy," said Mick. Ethan shook their hands. "This is Detective-Sergeant Ethan Cooper. He's former Special Air Service Regiment." Sam stepped forward and held out his hand to shake Ethan's.

"It's an honour to meet you, Sir," he said.

"Thank you, probie," said Ethan. He looked at Mick and whispered the words: "Sir?" Mick just shrugged his shoulders. Ethan just raised an eyebrow.

"So, what's the big emergency?" asked Diane.

"Detective Cooper is here because he has Intel on a possible terrorist threat…Ethan, want to break it down for us?" said Mick.

"A former squad member of my SASR unit, Alex Morgan, came to me this morning. He informed me that a domestic terrorist group is plotting to carry out an attack," said Ethan, "he gave me this portable hard drive containing encrypted data about who's behind the attack, and how it's being carried out." He then handed Mick the hard drive. Mick turned and gave it to Felicity. "Hey Felicity."

"Hey Ethan. Good to see you again," she said, and she smiled. As she connected it to her terminal, Mick continued to talk.

"Right now, our priority is protecting the memorial service. We've got less than an hour before it starts." He turned to Felicity. "So, what are we dealing with here?"

"Looks like it's a triple-layer encryption. It's going to take a while to decipher the code," she explained.

"How long is a while?"

"I'd say ten to fifteen minutes, tops," she said.

"Jesus, cutting it kind of close," said Ethan.

"I know, but it's the best I can do," she replied. Mick just nodded.

"Alright, keep at it. Let us know," said Mick. "In the meantime, I'll have a workstation set up for you."

"Thanks." Before he left, Mick's assistant came over to him.

"Chief Inspector, I just got a message from the Alfred Hospital. Alex Morgan is out of surgery," she said, and he nodded.

"That's a relief…You want to go and question him?" asked Mick. Ethan grinned.

"I thought you'd never ask," he said, and walked off.

There were already dozens of people at St. Mary's Cathedral. The family members of Prime Minister Harold Samson were standing in a group at the main entrance to the cathedral. They were all dressed in black and the prime minister's wife wore a black hat. She was trying very hard not to burst into tears, but she couldn't resist shredding a tear. Of course, the family had already arrived and were talking with several guests. The Premier of New South Wales had recently arrived, and he was offering his condolences. Members of the press were out the front taking photos and giving live press reports. A few moments later, several government vehicles arrived. They were sleek and shiny with a protection of police bikes and other vehicles. It was the incumbent Prime Minister of Australia, Stephen Brown. A body-guard opened the door and almost at the same time, the PM stepped out. The President of Australia Christine Mills was already there, and she stood amongst the grieving guests. News helicopters hovered over the St Mary's Cathedral, and were live streaming the funeral.

John Taylor couldn't believe what he'd just found out. He was on his way to Sydney Tower to meet with Andrew Shaw. The fact that Andy told him he was right about Amanda's suicide being faked was circling through his mind, and then the conversation he'd just had with Christine. He sat in the back seat of his escort vehicle. He was being driven by Mitch Clark. As he sat there, he could hear the radio, and it was giving a broadcast about the funeral service, stating that the Prime Minister of Australia had just arrived at the cathedral.

He knew he should have been there to support Christine, but this was just as important. The city was relatively empty, because most people were attending the funeral. While not everyone was able to be inside St. Mary's cathedral, hundreds congregated nearby in the streets.

John's escort vehicle pulled up and parked near the main entrance to the Sydney Tower. Mitch Clark got out and opened the door for him. "Are you sure this is a good idea, Sir?" asked Mitch.

"It will be fine, Mitch. Andy wanted to meet with me. I didn't pursue this," he said.

"I just think this guy is wasting your time." John smiled.

"I appreciate your concern. But it'll be fine," he said. He then headed up the stairs and went into the main foyer. After taking the elevator, he finally arrived at the tower's restaurant, which had a magnificent view of the city. There were only a handful of people in the restaurant, as they were all at the service. John spotted Andrew sitting at a table near a window. "Would you wait for me here, Mitch?" Of course, Mitch wasn't too keen on that idea.

"I'm not sure I'm comfortable with that, Sir."

"Please, Mitch. It's better this way…Besides, you can see me from the elevator," he said. Then Mitch nodded.

"Okay, call me if you need anything." John just smiled.

Then he walked over to where Andrew was sitting. He got up and seemed to be somewhat nervous.

"John, thanks for coming," he said.

"It's my pleasure...So, what's with all the cloak and dagger?"

"You know Amanda was an investigative journalist?" John slowly nodded. "Well, two months before her death, she came home one night to tell me that she was on the verge of publishing a major story. But she seemed terrified about it," he began.

"Terrified of what?"

"She said she found out that a private defence contractor was selling military-grade weapons to a criminal warlord in East Timor."

"Jesus...Who is this defence contractor?"

"She said it was Birchall McClelland. She had a source inside the company who confirmed the transactions, but the source ended up dead." John's eyes widened. He couldn't believe it. "It turns out that Birchall McClelland are against the idea of Australia being a republic. Amanda was days away from proving that the company was plotting something major."

"Oh, my God...They're the largest defence contractor in the Oceanic region," he said, and Andy nodded.

"She also found out the company was directly financing and supporting a terrorist group who were operating on Australian soil. They were financed to be a scapegoat, so BMC wouldn't be incriminated," he added.

"Do you know who this group was?"

"No, she never got that far. But she had enough evidence to publicly destroy the company ten times over...Someone must've found out what she was doing, and…Well, you know," he said, getting emotional and teary.

"I know, Andy. It's hard…You told me someone paid you off. Was it Birchall McClelland?"

"Yeah. Before she died, Amanda gave me the evidence she'd acquired against the company…BMC paid me a visit and offered me the two hundred thousand dollars in exchange for the evidence, and to keep my mouth shut, otherwise, they'd do the same thing to me." John didn't know what to say. "But, being intelligent as she was, Amanda made a backup copy of the evidence. It was hidden in a safety deposit box in her name. I only just found the key," he said.

"So, you have the evidence with you now?" Andrew looked around to check if they were being watched. Then, he produced a small thumb drive.

"This has the evidence against Birchall McClelland. If we can get this to the right people, we can bring these bastards to justice," he said.

"My God…And all this time I was forced to believe my daughter committed suicide," he said, as he sat there feeling overwhelmed by all of this.

"I know, I wanted to say something earlier, but I was afraid they were watching me," said Andy.

"It's okay, Andy. You did the right thing…I'm going to expose this evidence," he said, and Andy smiled.

Mitch Clark was standing by the elevator, watching as John was talking with Andrew Shaw. As he waited, he took out his mobile to dial a number.

"Yes?"

"It's Clark...We've got a problem."

"And that is?"

"John Taylor, the President's husband...He's looking into his daughter's suicide again. He's meeting with the fiancé, Andrew Shaw. I think he just gave him something that may be the evidence his daughter had," said Mitch. There was a slight pause.

"I thought we handle the Taylor situation?"

"I thought so too. But the fiancé approached him. If he goes public with that evidence, the company will be finished, Sir," said Clark.

"I'm aware of the consequences, Mr. Clark...See that the problem is taken care of." Mitch paused for a moment.

"Yes Sir, Mr. Benedict," he said, and then hung up. He continued to stand there and watch John talking with Andrew Shaw.

Felicity Meyers was getting impatient. She was frustrated because she was having difficulty with decrypting the hard drive. It was proving to be more of a challenge than she originally anticipated. But she was slowly getting through it. She'd spent the last ten minutes trying to get through the hard drive's secure firewall; she'd never seen anything like it before, though she was excited by the challenge. As she typed at her computer, Chief Inspector Mick Greer came over to her station. He was accompanied by Diane Faulkner. "Felicity, what's the status on the hard drive?" asked Mick, as they stood in front of her.

"I'm going as fast as I can. It's a highly secure drive with a Phoenix encryption. If I make one wrong move, it will erase the entire content of the hard drive," she explained.

"We don't need to hear all the technical babble, Felicity. Just do what you can to unlock that drive," said Mick. He looked over at Diane, who was becoming concerned.

Detective Sergeant Ethan Cooper arrived at the Alfred Hospital. He was accompanied by Detective Constable Sam Hunter. They just found out that Alex Morgan had woken up. He was still a bit out of it from his surgery, but they needed to talk to him as soon as possible. He had vital intelligence concerning a potential terrorist attack. Both made their way down the corridor and approached the nurse's station. Since Sam was the one who had any real authority, he smiled at one of the nurse's assistants, and presented his ID badge. "Hi there. I'm Detective Constable Sam Hunter with the Serious Crimes Unit. We need to speak with a patient of yours…Alex Morgan?" he said. The nurse checked her computer screen.

"Yes, of course. He's right down the corridor in room 4B," she said. Sam nodded. Ethan and Sam started walking. They finally got to the room and went in. Alex Morgan was only just conscious and connected to a respiratory machine to help him breath. "Bloody hell," said Sam, as he saw the condition he was in.

"Alex?" said Ethan, in a loud voice. He walked up to him. "Alex, can you hear me?" He didn't respond, but his fingers twitched. "Alex, it's Ethan Cooper...We need you to help us. You told me you have Intel on a terrorist attack. We're trying to access the hard drive you gave me, but it's encrypted...How is the attack being carried out?" he demanded, in a raised voice. Again, he didn't answer. Ethan just shook his head. "This is ridiculous." He went over and suddenly grabbed the tube that was providing him with morphine and squeezed it. Alex jumped awake, and the heart rate monitor started beeping rapidly.

"Sir, what the hell?" said Sam. He couldn't believe what he was doing.

"Start talking, Alex! How is the attack being carried out?" he shouted. Finally, he began to open his mouth in attempt to speak. "I can't hear you Morgan!"

"S-Shooter," he said, with great difficulty. Ethan's eyes widened with shock. "Son of a bitch." Realizing what he meant, Ethan quickly took out his mobile to start dialling a number.

"Mick Greer," he answered.

"It's me. I just questioned Alex Morgan. He said the attack is being carried out by an assassin. There must be someone nearby," he said. There was a sudden pause.

"Bloody hell…He must be trying to take out one or both leaderships."

"Yeah, I know. You have to evacuate the cathedral now!"

"I can't just authorize an evacuation. Besides, the service just started."

"Boss, if Alex is telling the truth, then the President's life is at stake," he said. He paused again.

"Alright, I'll alert the President's security detail, and authorize a counter-terrorist squad," he said. After he hung up, Mick quickly dialled another number. "This is Chief Inspector Mick Greer, SCU. I am issuing a code red emergency. Initiate a level one evacuation of St. Mary's cathedral, now!" he said. Superintendent Anna Mackenzie came over.

"Mick, what's going on?"

"Ethan just called. He said there's a threat to the memorial service," he said.

"What sort of threat?"

"It's a shooter," he said. She couldn't believe it. Her eyes widened with shock.

St. Mary's Cathedral was packed and the President of Australia, Christine Mills was sitting at one of the front seats with her Official Secretary, Joe Parsons, along with the Prime Minister of Australia, as well as his wife. The Premier of New South Wales was currently speaking. He was talking about how saddened he was by the loss of so many people. Since he was the Deputy Premier, he was elevated to the Premiership, after his predecessor was killed in the attack. "And to conclude, I offer my deepest sympathies to the family and loved ones of Mr. Samson...May God rest his soul," he said. Then he collected his notes and returned to his seat. Next, Christine got up to give her eulogy. Her hands were shaking as she got up to the main stage. She had a bit of a tear in her eye.

"Friends, family, loved ones and distinguished guests. Today is truly a solemn occasion. I come before you all, to pay tribute to a great man...Harold Samson," she began. "Harold Samson was this nation's Prime Minister...He was a great leader, and a well-respected person," she said, "I had the privilege of working with Prime Minister Samson, and during the short time I got to know him, I know for certain, that this country lost a brilliant leader," she said.

About a block away, a vehicle pulled up outside the main entrance to an apartment building. The building was several hundred metres away from St. Mary's Cathedral. The occupant of the vehicle got out, and he paid the taxi his fare. The man was carrying in his hand, a rectangular shaped case. He held onto it tightly and then made his way into the building. Upon entering, he got into an elevator, and it took him to the top floor of the building. The man was tall, about six foot four, in his mid-thirties, and wore a pair of dark coloured pants and khaki shirt. He also wore a black trench coat and a military vest underneath. He had a crew cut and a jiggered tattoo on the side of his neck. He was ex-military and now worked as a mercenary, probably for some defence contractor. The man stepped off the elevator. He made his way down the end of the corridor, where he came to the rooftop access door. There was a sign on it saying, 'Emergency Exit Only.' He pushed the door open and stepped out into the sunlight. He'd already had his sunglasses on, so the glaring sun didn't bother him. He walked over to the edge of the rooftop and placed the case down. He unlocked it and inside was a powerful looking sniper rifle; it was an Australian Army issued SR98. The weapon was disassembled in multiple sections, but since the man was ex-military, he knew how to put it together. The SR98 was a magazine-fed, bolt action, manually operated rifle, used by the Australian Army. It was fitted with a telescopic sight and had a 7.62 millimetre caliber. The rifle had a range of about eight hundred metres, which was more than enough for what he needed to achieve. It took less than thirty seconds for him to assemble the rifle. Once it was put together, he carefully inserted a single gold-plated bullet into the rifle's chamber. He then adjusted the scope and rested the rifle on the building's edge. As he looked through the scope, he had a clear view of the main entrance to the St. Mary's Cathedral. There were still dozens of people outside, waiting for the people to come out. But he was only interested in one of them.

DEADLOCK

The whole time this was happening, SCU Detectives Sam Hunter and Ethan Cooper had arrived at St. Mary's Cathedral. Ethan's heart was racing as he knew he was running out of time to stop the threat, that is if there was even a threat to begin with. He was scanning the crowd with his sharp eagle-eyes, checking for anyone with a weapon of some kind. So far, it all seemed normal. The President of Australia was finishing up her eulogy.

At last, the service was concluding, and everyone was making their way out of the cathedral. Christine Mills was one of the first people to step out into the day light. She was also accompanied by Joe Parsons, and the Premier of New South Wales. More people started piling out. Prime Minister Samson's wife and adult children were next. Then, the Prime Minister of Australia, Stephen Brown, emerged from the cathedral. He was shaking hands with several people and kissed the cheek of the prime minister's wife. Just then, there was a loud bang. Everyone froze. It was as though time itself stood still. A bullet struck the Prime Minister of Australia in the neck.

It was panic stations. SCU personnel were running around the Ops Centre trying to get on top of the situation. Everyone was in shock as they saw the dozens of news reports flashing in by the second and analysts were struggling to keep up to date. Felicity was at her station. She was somewhat teary as she watched a live video of the chaos. The video was made from an amateur and it was already accumulating hits on social media sites. Mick Greer came over and was about to address his team. "Alright folks, listen up!" he called out. Everyone turned to their boss. "We are in an emergency…A few moments ago, there was an assassination attempt on the Prime Minister. As of now, we have no idea who was responsible for this...We need to coordinate with local authorities to assist in dealing with this crisis. We're paid to get results, so, let's provide them...Let's go!" he said, and everyone went back to work. Mick walked over to Felicity who was still trying to process everything. "Felicity, are you okay?"

"Not really...I can't believe this is happening," she said. Mick slowly nodded.

"I know...We have to find out who was responsible for this assassination," said Mick.

"Ballistics are analyzing the scene as we speak. They should be able to get a trace on the bullet used, so, hopefully it'll source an origin," she said.

"Any luck with that hard drive?" he asked, changing the subject. But sadly, Felicity shook her head.

"No, the algorithm is still processing through the encryption," she said. Mick was quite frustrated.

"Son of a bitch." He turned and saw Anna Mackenzie coming out of her office. "Keep working on it," he added. Felicity nodded and went straight to work.

"I've just spoken with the Commissioner...The Prime Minister is in critical condition," said Anna. Mick's face turned white as a ghost.

"Shit," he cursed.

"He's been rushed to the Alfred Hospital for emergency surgery, but he's lost a lot of blood," said Anna. Mick didn't say anything after that. "I've also been informed that Deputy Prime Minister Allen Brady will be taking charge of the crisis," she added.

"Good. Any word on the President?" Anna paused for a moment.

"Yes, she's being taken back to the residence."

"That's good at least," said Mick.

"The Commissioner is furious that something like this happened, Mick," said Anna.

"I know. My team is working around the clock. We should have something within the hour," said Mick. Anna just stood there for a moment, still in complete shock that this happened.

"I want to find those people responsible for this, Mick…No matter what it takes," she demanded, and then walked off.

After the incident at St Mary's Cathedral, Christine Mills was rushed back to the Admiralty House. She was in utter shock that something like this happened, especially at a funeral service. Christine's escort vehicle pulled in through the main gates. As the vehicle came to a stop at the main entrance, Christine just sat there, motionless. Joe gently touched her on the shoulder. She jumped. "Ma'am, we're here," he said, softly. She unbuckled her seatbelt and got out. She hardly said a word the whole time they went inside. They finally got back to her office, and she slumped down in her chair, exhausted and in complete dismay about what happened. Joe followed in after her and closed the door. "Your Excellency, we really need to think about putting out a statement," said Joe. Christine slowly turned to him. Her face was covered in dust and she had several cuts on her face.

"How did something like this happen?" she said, softly. Joe didn't know what to say.

"We'll get to the bottom of this, Your Excellency," he said. "In the meantime, I'll have Chris write up a statement." He slowly stood up and walked to the door.

Former Australian Army Major-General George Stanley stepped off the elevator. General Stanley was in his late forties, and several years from hitting fifty. He was probably one of the youngest to make the rank of Major-General, but that's because he was a dedicated service man. That was until Australia became a republic; General Stanley was one of those people who hated the idea of the country being a republic. So much so that he chose to resign his post in the Australian Army. General Stanley was hired by Birchall McClelland to train other likeminded personnel. He made his way down the corridor that led him to a reception area. There was a woman behind the desk and she smiled at the General. She didn't even bother to stop him as she knew who he was. The General entered a large office. He had a meeting with the company's Chairman, Karl Benedict; a secret meeting which only he knew about. Karl Benedict was sitting at his large glass desk.

The TV was on and it displayed a news report on the assassination attempt on the Prime Minister of Australia. General Stanley stood there and waited as his boss had his chair turned away. "Are we on schedule?"

"Yes Sir. I've made all the arrangements. My men are prepared and ready to move," he said. Karl smiled at that.

"Good to hear." The chair swung around. Karl Benedict smiled at the General.

"The assassination was an apparent success," he said, pointing to the TV.

"It was...I received word that the Prime Minister is in critical condition. It's likely he will not survive the surgery," said Karl.

"I know. The President has been taken back to the residence," said the General. Karl didn't respond straight away.

"I'm aware. This is only Stage 1 of the operation," said Karl.

"Then I assume you're authorizing the secondary mission?" he asked.

"Of course, one way or another, I want this bitch dealt with," he said. General Stanley nodded. The room fell silent after that, and Karl looked back at the TV.

Christine Mills was in her office at the Admiralty House. She was still in shock that the attack happened and so many people were killed. She sat at her desk, attempting to write her speech to address the nation, but she just couldn't focus. She sat there with her pen in her hand, but as she went to write, she got the shakes and in frustration, she threw it down. The attack was all over the news. Every single news channel was broadcasting it and were saying something different. As she sat there watching, the door opened and came in. "Joseph, what's the latest?" she asked, muting the TV.

"I just spoke with the AFP Commissioner. The PM is undergoing surgery, but I've gotten word that his injury is quite severe," he said, and Christine closed her eyes, and a single tear trickled down her cheek. The room fell silent after that.

"What's the prognosis?" she asked.

"It's unclear at this point, but it doesn't look good," said Joe.

"I can't believe this...Do they know who's responsible?" she demanded, but Joe shook his head.

"No. The AFP is working with ASIO to tracking down the suspects," said Joe. Christine just let out a sigh. Just then, Brian Stedman came in.

"Ma'am, the Deputy Prime Minister is on the line," he said, and she nodded.

"Thank you, Brian," she said and then Brian closed the door. A few moments later, Christine picked up the phone. "Deputy Prime Minister, how are you?"

"Hello, Your Excellency. I'm glad to hear you're okay," said Allen Brady, the Deputy Prime Minister of Australia.

"Yes, thank you, Allen. I'm just a bit shaken up by the situation," said Christine. There was a sudden pause in the room.

"I can understand that…I heard that the Prime Minister is undergoing surgery," he said.

"Yes, he's in critical condition. His prognosis is yet to be determined, but it's apparent that he may not make it through." The line fell silent after that.

"That is unfortunate, Your Excellency…I want you to know that you have my full support during this troubling time," he replied.

"Thank you, I appreciate that, Deputy Prime Minister."

"Will you be making a statement?" he asked. Christine let out a sigh.

"Yes, I will be addressing the nation within the next hour," said Christine.

"Very well…Your Excellency, in light of this troubling situation, I feel that it be necessary that a state of emergency should be imposed, until we can get a handle on this crisis," he said. She paused after that and didn't know how to respond.

"Of course, that is a good idea, however, I will be leaving the decision up to the Premier. It is after all, the state that this incident occurred in."

"Your Excellency, with respect, this is a national emergency. Therefore the federal government should be in charge of dealing with the crisis," said the Deputy Prime Minister.

"It is a state matter, Deputy Prime Minister...The Premier is more than capable of dealing with this situation. I am keeping an open line to his office, and you'll be kept apprise of any developments," said Christine. There was a pause after that. Christine knew he wasn't happy by any of this. "I do appreciate your call, Deputy Prime Minister."

"Thank you, Your Excellency. Let me know if you need anything else," said Allen. Then she disconnected the call. She paused for a moment and looked up at Joe.

"Set up a press conference would you, Joe?" she requested, and he nodded.

Ethan couldn't believe what had happened at the funeral service. He was feeling partly responsible for it since he only just got the information from Alex in time. He had since returned to the agency after he wrongfully questioned Alex. Ethan was sitting around in the agency's briefing room. Reports of the assassination attempt were still being displayed. Aerial shots from a news helicopter showed the chaos that ensued at the cathedral. Just then, Mick Greer came in. "Any word on the Prime Minister?"

"He's still in surgery. Rumours are spreading that he's not going to make it."

"Look Mick, about Alex. I'm really sorry that he refused to give that Intel about the threat," he added.

"Don't worry about it, Ethan. It was out of your control. The important thing is, he came clean at the last second," said Mick. Just then, Felicity came barging in. She was carrying her hand-held tablet.

"Boss, preliminary results of the forensic analysis just came in," she said.

"What are we dealing with?"

"Ballistics confirmed the bullet was in fact Australian made," she said, "it's military issued. The bullet was paired with an Australian Army SR-98 bolt-action rifle," she said, and showed Ethan and Mick the tablet. There were images of the SR-98 sniper rifle, as well as video footage of it being fired.

"Shit. That's a pretty powerful weapon. Came across those when I was in the SASR. Those Army blokes used them in Afghanistan," said Ethan.

"Any idea where it came from?"

"It appears that this weapon was manufactured here in Australia," she said. Both Ethan and Mick looked at each other with shock. "I did some further investigation and discovered that aside from the Australian Defence Force, there's one other organisation that uses it," she said.

"And who's that?" asked Mick, becoming confused.

"Birchall McClelland," she said, bringing it up on the main screen. Mick's eyes widened.

"Bloody oath...The defence contractor?" Felicity slowly nodded. "I can't believe this...Alright, so we have to assume that the company was behind the assassination attempt...Where are they headquartered?"

"BMC have a corporate office downtown Sydney. At Grosvenor Place," she said. "The company is led by Karl Benedict, he's the Chairman of the Board."

"Alright...We're going to have to tread carefully here. Obviously, we can't just arrest the Chairman of an internationally renowned defence contractor without evidence."

"We also just can't ignore this. If the company was responsible for the assassination attempt on the Prime Minister, they must be held accountable," said Ethan.

"It makes sense...A defence contractor that large would have the means and the resources to pull off something like this," said Mick. He paused for a moment. "I'll have Diane and Sam go and question Benedict. Felicity, can you arrange an appointment with Benedict?" he asked, and Felicity slowly nodded.

After his meeting with Andrew Shaw, John was being driven across town by Mitch. John was still getting over the fact that he had evidence that proved Amanda was murdered. He was going to meet with someone that Mitch knew to hopefully unlock the mystery on the USB device. John sat in the back. He was watching a news report on the small TV he had on the back of the front seat. It was showing an update on the assassination attempt on the Prime Minister. The report was stating that authorities believed it to be a terrorist act. He had no idea what was happening with Christine, or if she was okay. They finally arrived at the location in Mascot. As the car stopped, Mitch got out and went to the back door to open it for John.

He stepped out and saw the large house. It was old and surrounded by trees and bushes. It had an over grown front lawn and a rusty old letter box. He was a little surprised that someone was living here by the state of the house. "So, who is this person we're meeting?" asked John, as they approached the front door.

"He's an old friend of mine. He's very resourceful when it comes to computers."

"Whoever it is, they obviously don't know how to maintain a house," said John. Mitch didn't say anything at first. He led John up the footpath.

"I'm sure he'll be able to help with your problem, Sir," said Mitch. They made their way up the front steps.

"I hope so. Because whatever is on this device will prove my daughter was murdered," he said.

"Sir, are you sure you want to go through with this?" he asked.

"Of course, Mitch. My daughter was murdered by these people...I'm going to make them pay," he said. Mitch didn't say anything after that. Mitch led him inside.

The house looked as though it had been abandoned for quite some time. There was no furniture, and sections of wallpaper were missing. "This place is a dump. Are you sure we're at the right address?" asked John. He turned around, and almost fainted as he saw a dead body on the ground. It was Andrew Shaw. He lay in a puddle of blood. "Oh, my God, it's Andrew!" John shouted and went over to help. "Mitch, call and ambulance!" he shouted. "Mitch, for God's sake, he needs help." But Mitch didn't reply. Just then, there was a clicking sound. John turned around and saw Mitch standing there with a gun aimed at him. He slowly got to his feet and raised his hands in the air. "Mitch, what the hell are you doing?"

"I'm sorry, Mr. Taylor...But you should've left it alone," said Mitch, as he held the gun at his face. John didn't know what to do. He just stood there, in complete shock. Sydney was in complete shock.

News reports of the assassination attempt were rapidly circulating, and many people were scared out of their minds, fearing that something else was going to happen. Many people were at home, as they were afraid to go out. SCU Detectives Sam Hunter and Diane Faulkner arrived at Grosvenor Place in downtown Sydney. Sam was driving, and he pulled up on the side of the road. They were both still in shock as they couldn't believe what had just happened. Sam put the vehicle in park and sat there for a moment, trying to calm himself. Diane looked over at him. "Are you okay?" she asked, noticing he was off with the fairies.

"Yes, sorry Dee. I just can't believe what happened," he said. Diane placed her hand on his shoulder.

"I know. It's a bit of a shock, but we've got to keep moving," she said. Sam unbuckled his seat belt.

"So, who is this guy we're meeting?" he asked.

"His name is Karl Benedict. He's the Chairman of Birchall McClelland, or BMC. HQ believes that he or someone in his company may be responsible for the attack," she said, as she scrolled down an intelligence report on her tablet. "Are you ready for this?" she asked, again.

"Yeah, I'm fine. Let's go," he said, and opened the door.

Together, they headed across the courtyard and made their way into the main foyer of Grosvenor Place. There weren't that many people about except for the odd security guard and employee. Sam and Diane approached the security desk. "Can I help you?" asked the service desk clerk.

"I'm Detective Sergeant Diane Faulkner, Serious Crimes Unit," she said. She showed the woman her ID badge. "We have an appointment with Karl Benedict of BMC." She smiled.

"Of course. Their offices are on the fortieth floor. I'll call reception and let them know you're here," she said. Diane smiled. They turned and headed over to the elevator.

"Is it just me, or does this place seem awfully quiet?" said Sam, in an audible tone. Diane didn't say anything. The elevator finally arrived at level forty. When they stepped off, the whole floor was quiet, dead quiet. They walked down the corridor and approached another reception desk. There was a blonde-headed woman behind the desk and she looked up as they approached. Diane got out her agency ID.

"Hi there, I'm Detective Faulkner. SCU. We have an appointment with Mr. Benedict," she said. The woman didn't respond. She just picked up her phone and dialled a number. A couple of seconds later, she got up and led them down another corridor. At the end, she knocked on a glass door and pushed it open. Diane smiled at the woman as they entered the large, spacious office. Karl Benedict was standing by the window, puffing on a cigar.

"Mr. Benedict, Detectives Faulkner and Hunter to see you," she said. They went in and the receptionist turned to leave.

"So, what can I do for the feds?" asked Karl, as he turned around and went over to his desk.

"Mr. Benedict, I'm Detective Faulkner. I'm sure you're aware of the assassination attempt on the Prime Minister?" she asked.

"Yes...It's such a tragedy...Have you found those responsible?" he thought.

"That's why we're here...My office believes that someone inside your organisation is directly supporting the shooter," she said. Karl's eyes widened.

"That is ridiculous...My company has no connection what so ever to any terrorists," he snapped. Diane looked at Sam.

"I realise this is difficult to understand, but we have reason to believe someone inside your company was directly responsible for the assassination attempt," said Diane.

"Detective Faulkner…This Company is an international renowned defence contractor. There are no terrorist connections!" he barked, standing up. Diane didn't say anything after that. "Now, unless you and your people have evidence to support such ludicrous accusations, I'd strongly suggest you two disappear back into the woodworks, you bloody spooks!" he said. His face was turning red with anger. Of course, Diane being as professional at her job, took the hint and got up from her chair.

"My apologies, Mr. Benedict. We're simply just trying to find out who is responsible for this atrocity," she said, and proceeded towards the door. "Detective Hunter, let's go." Sam stood up, but he didn't leave. He just stood there staring at Karl Benedict.

"I hope you're proud of yourself," he said. Karl looked up at him.

"Excuse me?"

"We know you're behind this…Stop playing games, Benedict! Tell me who you paid to carry out the assassination!" he shouted.

"Detective Hunter, that is enough!" Diane shouted.

"Detective Faulkner, kindly remove your colleague from these premises forthwith," he demanded.

"Detective Hunter, we need to leave." Sam continued to stare at Karl, wanting nothing more than to punch him in the face. But he came to his senses and listened to his superior officer. He started walking away. "I will be formally issuing a complaint against your detective and the AFP for its absurd accusations," he said. Diane hesitated and then they left. They made their way out and headed back to the elevator.

"What the hell do you think you're doing, Sam? I can't believe you said that to him!" she said, as they waited for the elevator.

"I had to say something, he's a guilty son of a bitch," said Sam.

"That doesn't matter! We can't just accuse him like that, we have protocols to follow," said Diane. "Come on." They stepped into the elevator. After they left, Karl Benedict was starting to get worried. Having two law enforcement officers in the office was somewhat concerning. He sat there for a moment, recovering from the unlawful interrogation, and then picked up his phone to dial a number.

"Yes?" a voice answered.

"It's me...I've just been interrogated by two AFP officers," said Karl.

"Son of a bitch...What did they want?"

"They said they have evidence someone in this company was directly responsible for the assassination of the Prime Minister," said Karl.

"My God...What kind of evidence do they have?"

"It's unclear…One of the officers accused me of being a criminal. I'll be issuing a complaint which should slow them down a bit, but it won't stop them," said Karl.

"I'd still like to know why they were questioning you about the shooting," he said.

"I've been thinking about that. It would seem we have a leak," he said.

"You think someone on our side spilled the beans to the authorities?" Karl didn't reply straight away.

"It's the only explanation…I have a feeling I know who it is…Alexander Morgan."

"Morgan? You think it was him?"

"It has to be…None of my subordinates have seen or heard from him in the last week," said Karl.

"This complicates things."

"I know…We're going to have to move up the time table…Continue with the operation as planned."

"It will be handled, Sir." Then the call disconnected. Karl hung up the phone and looked back at the TV which continued to show a live news report on the assassination attempt on the Prime Minister.

Christine and Joe were making their way down the corridor. She was about to give a live press conference outside the Admiralty House. Even though the Deputy Prime Minister had recently made a statement, as the nation's first President, she also gave speeches to voice her opinion on matters of national security. As they walked down the corridor, she was reviewing her speech and getting updates on the attack. "So, what's the latest on the PM?" she asked, as they walked.

"The surgeons are doing everything they can. The PM lost a lot of blood. They're finding it difficult to stop the bleeding." Christine closed her eyes.

"Damn it…Do we have any idea who was responsible?"

"The AFP suspect it may be an ex-military officer. Someone who is highly skilled, but obviously mentally unstable," said Joe. "They're keeping me up to date with their investigation." Christine smiled.

"Thanks Joe. I need you to schedule a meeting with the Deputy Prime Minister. I want to know what's being done to find the people behind this," she said. They made their way outside the main entrance of the residence. A group of reporters and journalists were waiting impatiently to get their story from the head of state. Christine approached the group of blood-thirsty reporters. "Good afternoon," she began. Cameras clicked, and microphones were shoved into her face. "Today, we suffered a tragedy. Earlier this morning, there was an assassination attempt on the Prime Minister…" cameras continued flashing as the President stood there, looking assertive. "Our thoughts and prayers are with the Prime Minister's family, and of course, to the family of prime minister Harold Samson," she said. She paused for a moment to collect her breath. "As President of Australia, I make it my firm promise to find and punish those responsible for this heinous atrocity," she said. No one spoke, and cameras continued flashing.

John Taylor was fearing for his life. He couldn't believe that his own body-guard was involved in the death of his daughter. John had been strapped to a chair and tape covered his mouth. Mitch Clark was starting to panic. He'd been calling a number for the past five minutes, but no one seemed to be picking up. Finally, someone answered. "Yes?"

"Mr. Benedict, it's Mitch Clark," he said.

"What's going on, Clark? Has the problem been taken care of?" asked Karl Benedict.

"Not yet. I have Taylor in the safe house…Do you really think it's necessary for me to kill him?"

"Of course, it is. It has to look like John Taylor murdered the fiancé, and then killed himself," said Karl, "is that so difficult to understand?" Mitch didn't reply straight away and looked back at John who was still tied to the chair. "Mr. Clark?"

"Yes, Sir. I understand…It'll be taken care of," he said, and then hung up the phone. Mitch walked over to John who was shaking. He ripped off the tape from John's mouth.

"Damn it, Mitch. You're a son of a bitch," he cursed. "You killed my daughter!"

"I'm sorry, Mr. Taylor. Your daughter was looking into things she wasn't supposed to be," he said, as he walked around the room.

"You didn't have to kill her!"

"She was on the verge of discovering the truth about the people I work for. They weren't prepared to let that truth be exposed," said Mitch.

"The people you work for? They're criminals Mitch!"

"See, that's where you're wrong. These people are masterminds. They see what this country really is…Pathetic," he said.

"That still doesn't justify murder," said John.

"Unfortunately, your daughter inherited your determination...And that's why you'll have to be silenced, just as she was."

"You're never going to get away with this, Mitch. I'm a public figure. People will ask questions, and when the dust settles, all the blame will fall on you," said John. Mitch didn't say anything after that, he just stared at John.

"If it's any consolation, Sir. Your daughter died quickly, and painless," he said. He held a handgun and aimed it at John's chest. The gun had a suppressor to block the noise of the gunshot. Mitch held his hand on the trigger and prepared to fire.

Christine Mills was back in her office at the residence. She had just given a public statement and expressed her concerns and outrage about the situation. She was still in utter shock about it. It had been several hours since the assassination attempt, and all that time, news stations across the nation were reporting on what happened. They were speculating as to who was responsible, and some news channels were suggesting that it was the works of a UAG terrorist cell. There were also reports about the President's statement she recently made and indicated that she was determined to bring those responsible to justice. Christine stood by the window and looked out across the city. It was late afternoon and the sun was starting to set. As she stood there, she looked over her shoulder as there was a knock at the door. "Come in," she called out. Then, Joe Parsons entered. He too was in shock. "Oh, afternoon Joe."

"Afternoon, Ma'am. How are you feeling?" he asked. He kind of already knew the answer to that question.

"I'm alright, Joe. Just in complete shock by all of this," she said. "What's happening with the AFP's investigation?" she went over to sit down at her desk. At the same time, she took a sip of her cup of tea.

"I've just got off the phone with the AFP Commissioner. He's in charge of counter-terrorism operations. According to him, they have a possible suspect behind the assassination attempt," he said. Christine's eyes widened.

"Well, that's great. Who do they think was behind it? The UAG?" she thought, but Joe shook his head.

"No...The AFP suspect it was the workings of a private defence contractor...Birchall McClelland," he said. Christine's eyes widened.

"Oh my, God...Are you saying the AFP think this defence contractor was responsible for the assassination attempt?"

"It looks that way. They have detectives investigating it as we speak."

"I can't believe this...I don't understand, what a private defence contractor would gain from killing the Prime Minister?" she said.

"I have absolutely no idea...But we'll soon find out. The Commissioner is keeping me apprised of any updates on the investigation," he added, and Christine nodded. Just then, there was another knock at the door. Her executive assistant, Brian Stedman entered.

"Yes Brian?" she asked.

"Your Excellency, the Premier of New South Wales is on the phone," he replied. Christine nodded.

"Thank you, Brian," she said. She then picked up the phone. "Premier, thank you for taking my call."

Detectives Diane Faulkner and Sam Hunter returned to SCU. They'd just got back from questioning Karl Benedict, the Chairman of Birchall McClelland. Sam was quite frustrated by the fact that Karl Benedict lied to their faces, and that he denied the allegations that he was supporting terrorists. Both Diane and Sam made their way across the floor and went over to the briefing room. Inside, Ethan and Mick were standing over the table and working through stacks of paper work. "Hey Boss, just letting you know we're back," said Detective Faulkner.

"Good. How'd it go at BMC?" he asked.

"Not well…Benedict denied the allegations. He was somewhat nervous when we mentioned the fact that his company was helping terrorists," Diane explained. Mick rolled his eyes.

"Figures...While you were gone, Felicity managed to unlock part of the encrypted hard drive Ethan got from Alex Morgan," he explained.

"That's great. What did you find?"

"So far, we've managed to recover a large chunk of Birchall McClelland's corporate financial records. We've got bank transfers, corporate accounts, deposits...All dating back two months ago. Most of it's insignificant, but we managed to find several transactions made by the company's Chief Financial Officer. We've identified several real-estate properties purchased by BMC."

"How many are there?" asked Diane.

"We've identified six. Most are scattered about the country, but there's one here in Sydney...It's a house in Mascot," said Mick. "We found out the company purchased it more than two months ago," said Ethan.

"So, you think BMC leased this house to the Universal Adversary Group?" said Diane, and Mick slowly nodded.

"We're putting together a tactical operation plan as we speak. Felicity has a drone circling overhead. I'm sending Ethan and Sam with a tactical-ops unit to the location," said Mick.

"Alright, let's move out. Sam, you're with me," said Ethan, as he headed to the door.

After a short drive, the SCU tactical operations unit arrived in the suburb of Mascot, which was nearby Sydney airport. Ethan Cooper sat in the front seat of an SCU Range Rover. Detective Constable Sam Hunter was driving, and he pulled up alongside the tactical ops vehicles. They were about a block away from the target house, the suspected Universal Adversary Group's headquarters. It was a large four-bedroom house and blended in with the neighbourhood. Ethan and Sam got out of the vehicle and walked over to where the other AFP officers were gearing up and getting ready to raid the house.

At the SCU, Mick and the others stood by Felicity's desk as she was controlling a surveillance drone. It was hovering over the area where Ethan was. "Alright, gents. This is what we have," said Ethan. "We have a suspected terrorist cell residing in this residential house. We believe these terrorists to be responsible for the attack on the memorial service earlier this morning," he said. "Infra-red scanning indicates there are four potential hostiles inside the residence, and they may be armed, so we have to breach the premises with extreme caution," he added. "Our priority is to capture one if not all hostiles alive. They have vital information relating to our investigation...Right, you have your mission profile, let's move out," he said. Then, both Ethan and Sam withdrew their Glock 19 handguns and cocked them. The twelve-man assault unit started making their way down the footpath towards the target house. As they closer to the main entrance, two of the officers advanced to the front door. One of them had a protective shield and guarded the other officer as he planted a small plastic explosive on the door. They took a step back and the officer detonated the explosives. The front door burst open.

At that, twelve counter-terrorist officers stormed the house, along with Ethan and Sam. They searched all the rooms in the house except for one. An officer busted the door down with a battering ram, and Ethan and Sam stormed the room, along with six armed officers. In the middle of the room was a man standing there holding a gun. It was pressed against the head of John Taylor, the President's husband.

"Drop your guns, or I pull the trigger!" the man shouted, as he held his finger on the trigger. John was quivering as he'd been tied to the chair and his mouth had been gagged. Both Ethan and Sam stood there with their Glock 19's aimed at the man.

"Take it easy...There's no way out of this," said Ethan. "Just put your weapon down and put your hands on your head." The man just ignored them and prepared to pull the trigger; at that, one of the counterterrorist officers fired a shot. The man was shot in the shoulder, knocking him to the ground. Within a split second, the officers swarmed the armed man, and secured the hostage. Ethan was quite surprised at the fact that it was the President's husband, but he was unconscious. "Jesus...We need a medic in here now!" he shouted. "Sam, secure the hostage." Sam nodded, and went over to John Taylor. Ethan took out his mobile phone and started dialling a number.

"Mick Greer."

"Hey, it's me. We just raided the UAG safe house," said Ethan.

"What did you find?"

"There were four hostiles inside. We rescued a hostage, and took a hostile into custody," he said.

"Bloody hell. Who was the hostage?" asked Mick, becoming confused. There was a slight pause in the conversation.

"It was John Taylor…The President's husband."

"Jesus…How the hell did he get kidnapped?"

"I've got no idea, but the kidnapper looks like his personal body-guard. This conspiracy seems to be deeper than we thought."

"I can't believe this…Alright, what's Mr. Taylor's condition?"

"He's unconscious. Paramedics are here working on him, but I think they're taking him to RPAH."

"Okay, fine. What about the hostile?" asked Mick. "He's been shot. If he's involved in this, then he may have Intel on who's responsible for the attack," said Ethan.

"That's what I was thinking…Have him brought back here. I want him treated and prepped for questioning," said Mick.

"Got it. We're on our way." Then Ethan hung up.

It had been a long, tiring day for the President of Australia, Christine Mills; a day of sadness and chaos. She was trying to get over the fact that an Australian defence company wanted the Prime Minister dead. Christine was standing by the window of her office at the residence. It was just on dusk and the sun began to set behind the horizon. The city's lights were gradually turning on. She leaned against the railing and was lost in deep thought. She was thinking about how tough the campaign had been and was looking forward to seeing the end of this horrible day. The TV was on in her office and it continued to show a report on the attack.

As she stood there, Joe Parsons knocked on the door and let himself in. He saw her standing by the window. "Everything alright, Your Excellency?" he asked, as he closed the door. Christine looked over.

"Oh, yes Joe. Sorry, I was just thinking about everything." Joe smiled.

"That's understandable...The AFP just faxed over the latest report," said Joe, as he held a manila folder. But he could see that she was distressed by the whole thing. "We can do it another time if you like."

"No, Joe it's fine. What are the numbers?" she asked, putting on her reading glasses.

"Well, total estimates place fifty-one casualties, at least twenty critically injured," he said, reading over the report.

"I didn't realise it was that many," she said, suddenly becoming overwhelmed.

"Shall I continue?" he asked, and Christine nodded. "The AFP have finished securing the building. Criminal investigators are conducting a full investigation into the cause of the explosion," said Joe. "However, the AFP's Serious Crimes Unit has determined it was an act of terrorism," he explained, and Christine nodded. "I also received word from the Attorney-General's office that a warrant was issued. It appears that BMC were responsible for the bomb attack," said Joe. Christine's eyes widened.

"Bloody hell…You mean, they killed all those people?" Joe slowly nodded. "Yes. It's unclear who exactly was involved in this conspiracy, but the AFP is investigating as we speak," he replied. Christine didn't know what to say after that. Just then, there was a knock at the door. "Yes?" Brian Stedman poked in.

"Your Excellency, the AFP Commissioner is here to see you. He says it's regarding your husband," said Brian. Christine looked at Joe, confused.

"Send him in." Brian nodded, and opened the door to allow the Commissioner to step in. "Commissioner, please come in. Can I offer you something to drink?" she asked.

"No, thank you, Your Excellency. I'm afraid this isn't a social call. It's regarding your husband, John Taylor." The Commissioner was also accompanied by a senior detective. She looked at him confused.

"What's going on with John?" she demanded.

"Your Excellency, about ten minutes ago, counterterrorism officers raided a house in Mascot. We believe the house was a terrorist stronghold, and upon searching the house, we found your husband, John Taylor. It appears he'd been kidnapped and taken to the house...He was found along with the body of another man, Andrew Shaw. Do you know this person, Your Excellency?" asked the detective. Christine paused, and didn't reply straight away.

"Yes...It's my ex-son in law," she said, her eyes filling with tears. She couldn't believe what she was hearing. "Commissioner, how on earth did my husband get kidnapped?" she demanded.

"We're still looking into that Your Excellency, but the kidnapper appears to be Mr. Taylor's private bodyguard, Mitchel Clark," he explained.

"My God...Is my husband okay?"

"Yes, he's being taken to RPAH. He was unconscious when we found him...Ma'am, you should know, Mr. Clark has been taken into custody. Detectives are questioning him as we speak," said the Commissioner.

"Good. I want that bastard to pay for what he's done to my husband," she demanded.

"Don't worry Ma'am, we'll make sure he pays...We'll keep you updated." Then the call disconnected. Christine just sat there, shocked by all of this.

"Unbelievable...I'd like to know what my husband's been getting himself into," she said. Joe smiled. "Also, I want to find out the names of those officers who rescued John…I want to award them for their efforts."

"Of course, I'll get right on it." Joe stood up and left.

Ethan and Sam returned to the SCU office. They were still surprised at the fact that they just rescued the President's husband. More to the point, they couldn't believe he'd been kidnapped. As Ethan and Sam walked across the floor, they were greeted with an applause by all their colleagues, who'd just found out what they did. Sam was a bit overwhelmed by all of this, mostly because it was his first day. They made their way over to the main floor and shook hands with co-workers. Mick Greer was standing there along with Felicity Meyers and her team. They were all clapping with excitement. "Magnificent work, you two. Very well done," said Mick.

"Thanks Boss. We didn't know the President's husband had been kidnapped," said Ethan.

"Even still, you rescued him…And it probably won't go unnoticed," said Mick. Ethan just smiled.

"What's happening with the suspect?" he asked.

"He's in the clinic. Doctors are working on him as we speak," said Mick.

"Okay, we'll need to question him as soon as possible."

"I know, slow down buddy. I've put Faulkner on the interrogation." Ethan didn't say anything after that. Just then, Superintendent Anna Mackenzie came walking over. She walked over to where Ethan and Mick were standing.

"Excellent work Detective Cooper, Detective Hunter," said Anna. "I've just been talking with the Commissioner. He informed the President about her husband's kidnapping. Apparently, the President wants to award you for rescuing John Taylor." Both Ethan and Sam looked at Mick.

"Don't blame me, I didn't do anything," he said, with a grin.

"The President is expecting you both at the Admiralty House within the next hour to present you with the medals. So, I suggest you get yourselves cleaned up and get over to Kirribilli," she said, and then walked off. Ethan didn't know what to say to that.

Detective Sergeant Diane Faulkner was an expert at interrogations. She knew all the right questions to ask and certainly knew how to push the buttons of suspects. Mitchell

Clark had been taken to one of the SCU's interview rooms. It was a medium-sized room with a table in the middle of it. Mitchell Clark was sitting in the seat on the other side of it. To left of the table was a double-sided window; Diane Faulkner stood watching Mitch Clark in the observation room. As she stood there watching, the room's door opened, and Mick Greer stepped in. "How are we going?" he asked, as he stood next to Diane.

"He's all set up for the interview. We've got thermal detection software set up, he's also connected to a lie detector," she said.

"Okay...Felicity just finished doing the profile on him."

"What do I need to know?" she asked.

"His name is Mitchell Clark. Forty-two years old, university graduate, served in the Australian Army. He was then employed as a private security body-guard through Birchall McClelland...He was sub-contracted to protect the President's husband last year because Mr. Taylor was receiving death threats," he explained. "We also managed to pull his medical records...Seems he's being treated for a mental illness. Must've got that after the Army." Diane rolled her eyes.

"Great...So, we're dealing with a bonified nutcase," she said.

"Yes, well, this bonified nutcase is our only lead to uncover this conspiracy," said Mick.

"Alright fine. He's been sweating enough, I'm going in," said Diane. She went over and opened the door that led her into the interview room. Mitch didn't even look up as she entered. She went over and sat down on the chair opposite Mitch. She opened the folder and began to read his profile. "Interesting profile, Mr. Clark," she said. Of course, Mitch remained silent. She looked up at the gunshot wound. "That wound looks painful…I hope you're enjoying that pain relief the doctors gave you, because you're not getting any more unless you cooperate with me," she said. "So, why don't we start by telling us what your connection to Birchall McClelland is?" she said. "Who hired you to kidnap the President's husband?" Mitch slowly looked up at Diane. He was still very groggy from the procedure he endured.

"I was held captive by the Taliban for six weeks in Afghanistan. They tried everything to break me, but they didn't…You really think an underpaid cop like you can?" he said.

"First of all, I'm a detective…Second of all, I don't think those towel heads knew how to interrogate a prisoner," she said. "All I want to know is, why Birchall McClelland wanted to kidnap the President's husband!" she demanded, in a raised voice. Mitch just grinned.

"Alright, fine. I'll tell you…On one condition," he said.

"You're unbelievable…You're in no conditions to be making demands."

"You want to find out the truth?" Diane didn't reply straight away.

"What do you want?"

"I want a get-out-of-jail-free card signed by the Attorney-General...You get me that, then I'll tell you everything you want to know," he explained. Diane stared at him, not knowing whether to believe him. She sat there for a moment, and then stood up.

"Sit tight, I'll be right back." Then she disappeared into the observation room. "Can you believe this son of a bitch?" she cursed, as she approached Mick.

"I know. But he obviously knows something."

"Boss, he kidnapped the President's husband. I really don't think he deserves to be let go!" she said.

"Regardless, we need to find out what's going on. Birchall McClelland obviously have something sinister planned, and he's our best chance at stopping them," said Mick. Diane just stood there, frustrated by what she was hearing.

"Fine, if that's what you think is going to work."

"I do...I'm going to talk to Mackenzie. In the meantime, keep an eye on him," said Mick. He then headed to the door. He made his way across the floor and then approached the large executive office of Superintendent Anna Mackenzie. She was in her office catching up on some paperwork. Mick knocked on the glass door and showed himself in.

"Yes, Mick. Do come in. I'd like to know how the interrogation is going," she said.

"That's what I came to talk to you about...Detective Faulkner just finished questioning him. Apparently, he won't give up any information unless his demands are met."

"I see. And what are those demands?"

"He wants an immunity deal signed by the Attorney General," he said. Anna closed her eyes.

"That figures…What guarantee do we have that he'll give up his information?"

"Right now, he's our best chance at stopping the UAG. Clearly, he knows something about their plans, so we don't have much choice," said Mick. Anna sat there and thought about what to do.

"I don't like the idea of allowing this criminal to walk free. Especially since he did kidnap the President's husband."

"I know. But if the UAG is planning something, then more lives are at risk…We have to consider what's best for this country," said Mick. "Alright. I'll contact the Attorney-General. But I can't guarantee he'll sign off on the release," she said, and then picked up the phone.

It was just on seven o'clock in the evening. The sun had well and truly gone down, and Sydney was in darkness. The city was lit up by its brilliantly lit buildings. There were pleasure yachts in the bay and couples were enjoying a nice elegant meal. Further up the bay, there was an island which was referred to as Cockatoo Island. Once used as a prison during the days of the British Empire, it was since converted into a shipping yard. It was until recently abandoned and turned into a heritage site and a common tourist attraction. But today, it was being used by a group of men. This particular group were mercenaries and employees of Birchall McClelland, led by Major-General George Stanley. General Stanley was standing against the railing and looked out across the bay towards the city skyline. The General, a man in his mid-forties, was clearing his mind before he and his men were to carry out one final mission. His men, a group of six highly trained para-military officers, were gearing up and getting ready to leave. They'd been loading their equipment and weapons into a black rubber zodiac.

As the General stood there finishing his cigarette, one of his men, Lieutenant Carson came up to him, and stood to attention. "General Sir, the boat is loaded and ready to ship off," he said. General Stanley put out the cigarette and turned to face his officer. He then grinned.

"Good. Then let's move out," he said. After squishing the cigarette with his boot, he headed over to the zodiac where the other men were waiting. "Gentlemen, we're heading out." The men climbed into the zodiac. As they did so, General Stanley took out his phone to dial a number. "It's me. We're just about to leave."

"Excellent. How long before you get to the target?"

"We should be there in less than ten minutes," he replied.

"Good. No more communication until after the target is secured. Good luck, General." The General grinned.

"Thank you, Mr. Benedict," said Stanley, and hung up. After he did so, he climbed into the boat and it slowly sped off. The boat skimmed across the blackened waters of Port Jackson and was heading in the direction of the city.

Detective Sergeant Ethan Cooper and Detective Constable Sam Hunter had never been more nervous. Ethan hadn't felt like this since his wedding which was more than twenty years ago. They were about to meet for the first time, the President of Australia. Ethan and Sam had just arrived in Kirribilli after a ten-minute drive. They were sitting in the back seat of a black Range Rover Sports. Detective Constable Sam Hunter wore a black suit and black tie since it was a formal event, while Ethan wore his black suit. The Range Rover pulled into the main drive of the Admiralty House. It slowed down and stopped in the front courtyard. The President's Official Secretary, Joe Parsons was standing there waiting to greet them.

Ethan and Sam got out and buttoned their jackets. "Good evening, gentlemen. Welcome to the Admiralty House...I'm Joe Parsons, Official Secretary to Her Excellency, the President of Australia," he said. They both shook his hand. "The President is waiting for us in the main Dining Room, so if you'd like to follow me?" said Joe. He then escorted them inside the residence. Sam was impressed by the décor of the Admiralty House, since it was his first time being here.

"How is the President?" asked Ethan, as they headed into the residence.

"She's fine," said Joe. They came to a door. Joe knocked and then pushed it open. "Your Excellency, Detective Constable Samuel Hunter, Serious Crimes Unit, and Detective Sergeant Ethan Cooper," he said. Joe showed them in. Her

Excellency, Christine Mills turned around and smiled at them as they walked over to her.

"Gentlemen, thank you for coming. I just want to say how grateful I am for your efforts today," she said.

"It's our pleasure, Your Excellency," said Ethan. They both shook her hand. She looked over at Joe, and he nodded.

"With the power vested in me, as President of the Republic of Australia, I hereby bestow you both with the Australian Cross of Valour, for your acts of conspicuous courage in circumstances of extreme peril," she said. Joe handed her two rectangular shaped boxes. She opened them revealing the Cross of Valour medals. Sam's face was literally turning bright red. He was as nervous as ever, more so than when he proposed to his fiancé. Christine picked up one of the medals and pinned it on Ethan's jacket. They then shook hands. Christine picked up the next one and did the same thing for Sam. Sam shook hands with the President, and she smiled.

Superintendent Anna Mackenzie had just gotten off the phone with the Attorney-General of Australia. It wasn't a particularly pleasant conversation, and not one she wished to endure. Mick Greer was standing there waiting to hear the verdict of the conversation. "I take it the call didn't go well?" he asked. Anna just raised her eyebrow.

"What do you think?" she said. "He wasn't at all pleased by the fact that the man who kidnapped the President's husband was demanding to be released...However he wasn't prepared to allow another terrorist attack to take place…He granted the release," she said, and Mick nodded.

"That's good. When's it getting here?"

"It's being faxed over as we speak." Just then, Anna's assistant came in. She handed her a folder.

"This just came in from the Attorney-General's Department," she said, and quickly left. Anna opened the official looking folder and saw that it was a signed document stating that Mitchell Clark was a free man. She went to hand it to Mick.

"This had better be worth it, Mick. Otherwise, there will be hell to pay," she said. Mick took the folder.

"I hope so too."

Then he headed out the door. Carrying the folder in his hand, Mick made his way down the stairs and quickly rushed over to the observation room. Diane Faulkner was waiting there patiently and continued to stare at Mitchell. "Here it is. Clark's get-out-of-jail-free card," he said. He gave Diane the folder. Of course, she didn't say anything to Mick, as she was still pissed at him. Then she headed back inside the interview room.

"It seems to be your lucky day…I have a document signed by the Attorney-General stating that you are free to go," said Diane. Mitch grinned. "Now it's your turn to hold your end of the deal."

"Very well…What do you want to know?" he asked.

"What is the UAG planning next?" she demanded. Mitch didn't reply straight away. He hesitated and looked up at the clock on the wall. It was a few minutes past eight o'clock at night.

"The UAG are plotting an attack on the Admiralty House. Since they've already neutralized the Prime Minister, their next target is the President of Australia," he said. Diane's eyes widened.

"How are they carrying it out?"

"A hit squad is moving in on the House. They plan to take her out," he said. She couldn't believe it.

"How do I know this is true?"

"Because I sold detailed plans and blueprints of the Admiralty House to the UAG," he said. "Check my phone. They should be in there." Diane got up and went over to a bench. There was a tray with Mitchell's personal effects. She picked up the Smartphone and checked its photos. Sure enough, there was an image containing the blueprints of Admiralty House.

"My God," she said. She then rushed over to the observation room. As she opened the door, Mick was already on the phone giving orders.

"This is Mick Greer. I want a counter-terrorist unit dispatched to Kirribilli now, we are in a code-red," he said.

"Isn't Ethan and Sam at the Admiralty House?" said Diane. Mick paused for a moment. He then picked up his phone and started dialling a number.

"Shit...Ethan's not picking up," he said. He then started dialling another number. "Yes, this is Mick Greer, Serious Crimes Unit. I need to speak with the President's Official Secretary, urgently," he said. His call was then transferred. "Diane, get yourself over there." She nodded and then left.

"Joe Parsons."

"Mr. Parsons, this is Chief Inspector Mick Greer, Serious Crimes Unit. You have two of my people there, I need to speak with Detective Cooper now."

"I believe he's in a meeting with the President."

"I know. But there's been a security threat to the residence. I need to speak with him now," he demanded.

"Hold on just a moment." Joe went over and knocked on the door. He went in and Ethan and Sam were sitting down at the table talking with the President.

"Yes, Joe?" he asked.

"Sorry to interrupt, Ma'am. Detective Cooper, I have a Mick Greer on the phone, he says it's urgent," said Joe. Ethan got up and walked over to Joe. He took the phone and stepped out into the corridor.

"Hey Boss, it's Ethan. What's going on?" he asked.

"Ethan, thank God. Diane just interrogated Mitch Clark. He said that the UAG are planning to assassinate the President...He sold blueprints of the Admiralty House to the UAG. There's a hit squad coming in."

"Jesus. Is this for real?"

"Yes, they'll be there any second. You have to get the President to safety," he said.

"Bloody hell. Is tactical response on its way?"

"Yeah, I sent Diane with a tactical unit," he replied.

"Okay fine, I'll take care of the President. Just get those units here ASAP."

Just then, the call was distorted by static. "Boss, did you hear me?" he said, but there was nothing. "Son of a bitch." Ethan went back into the room. "Your Excellency, we need to get you to safety. There's been a threat to the building," said Ethan. His eyes widened.

"My God...What kind of threat?"

"There's a hit squad on its way, they're trying to kill you," he said. Sam immediately stood up and withdrew his Glock 19 handgun.

General Stanley and his team of mercenaries finally made it to Kirribilli Point. The zodiac they were in gently pulled up alongside the Admiralty House' private boat dock. There were several body-guards patrolling the dock, but they were completely unaware of the mercenaries. They were all taken out one by one with silenced weapons. The group advanced up the cobblestone steps that led them to the front of the house. There were several more body-guards patrolling the front porch. As they went to withdraw their weapons, they were immediately taken down. It was dark, but with the night vision goggles, they could move freely. The mercenaries were armed to the teeth with assault rifles and were combat-ready. Lieutenant Greg Carson took the lead and they proceeded into the residence. They smashed through one of the windows and took out a few more body-guards. They then proceeded up the stairs. Ethan and Sam were heading in the same direction and came face to face with the hit squad. They immediately open fired at Ethan. He started firing back, and as they did so, they began to move backwards; they were literally pressed up against the wall and took advantage of the darkened corridors. Outside, several AFP tactical vehicles pulled up and a team of officers were preparing to move in.

Detective Sergeant Diane Faulkner was amongst them, and she was getting herself ready to join the siege. As the gunfight continued, General Stanley and his men were advancing towards the President. The General fired a shot and hit Ethan in the shoulder. At that point, the General took advantage and quickly moved in on the President. He grabbed hold of her. "I have the President!" General Stanley shouted. The gunshots seemed to have stopped. Sam's heart was racing as he stood there aiming his gun at the General. Ethan was on the floor, clutching his gunshot wound, but he managed to slowly get to his feet. He was bleeding profusely.

"They've got the President," Sam whispered.

"Come any closer and I'll kill her!" said the General. He started moving back towards the other stairs. Despite having a bullet in his arm, Ethan and Sam moved closer to the General. Outside, an AFP tactical sniper was laying down on the ground. Using night vision, he had his scope aimed at the window on the second floor and could see the General holding the President at gunpoint.

"I have a clean shot on the hostile. Repeat, I have a clear shot. Do I proceed?" he asked, through his radio.

"Stand by," came the reply. Ethan and Sam both had their guns trained at the General and their fingers were gently pressed against the triggers.

"You come any closer, I will kill her!" the General shouted.

"Ethan, say the word," said Sam.

"Just give it a second," Ethan replied. "There's no way out of this! You are surrounded!" Ethan called out.

A helicopter was hovering overhead, and its spotlight beamed down, lighting up the corridor. Making their way up the stairs was a twelve-man counter-terrorist assault unit. One of them had a tactical shield used to deflect bullets. They were getting ready to move in. "I'm not going to say it again...Drop your weapons!" the President shouted, again. Sam was starting to worry. He was sweating. "Just let the President go now, and we can cut a deal," said Ethan, as he stepped forward slightly.

"This bitch is going down!" he said. He lifted his gun and was about to pull the trigger. Within a split second, a shot was fired, and a bullet struck the General in the neck. He let go of the President and fell backwards to the floor. He was shot by the sniper. At that, the assault unit moved in and immediately secured the President. Ethan lowered his gun and collapsed to the floor. Now that it was all over, he passed out due to the significant blood loss.

12 Hours Later.

News of the assassination attempt on the Prime Minister had shocked the entire nation. Surgeons did everything they could to save the Prime Minister. Sadly, at 06:05 hours this morning, the Prime Minister of Australia died. It was a tragic loss, having lost a second prime minister in the space of six months. The nation was grieving for the loss, and thoughts and prayers were being sent to the Prime Minister's family. All morning, the nation had been talking non-stop about the attack at the Admiralty House, and stating it was a secondary terrorist attack. Christine Mills, the President of Australia had returned to Canberra. She was still in utter shock by what had happened in Sydney, and the fact that she'd survived a catastrophic terrorist attack. She was sitting in her private study at the Government House in Canberra. As she sat there watching the news, there was a knock at the door. Her Official Secretary, Joe Parson's entered. "Oh, hi Joe. Come in." Joe noticed that the TV was on and it was showing a report on the attack on Admiralty House. "What's the latest, Joe?" she asked.

"I've just spoken with the AFP Commissioner. He's informed me that the terrorists responsible for yesterday's tragedy have been apprehended and taken into custody," said Joe.

"Oh, that is such good news…What about John? Have you heard from the hospital?" she asked.

"Yes, I spoke with the doctors. John is going to pull through. He's expected to make a full recovery," said Joe. Christine was relieved. "Your husband is a fighter, Ma'am."

"I know. I just wish I'd listened to him when he came to me with all of this," she said. "I still can't believe that someone murdered Amanda," said Joe. There was a brief pause in the conversation, and Joe slowly nodded.

At Sydney Hospital, Detective Sergeant Ethan Cooper was recovering from the gunshot wound. He'd just come out of surgery and was back in his room. As he regained consciousness, Chief Inspector Mick Greer was there. "Hey. Welcome back to the land of the living," he said, with sarcasm. "How are you feeling?" he asked.

"Ugh, like I've been shot," he said, Mick just chuckled. "What happened? Is the President okay?" he asked, getting excited.

"Relax, buddy. It's all over. He's safe. Also, the AG determined that BMC was responsible for the memorial attack...The Company has been shut down, and Karl Benedict is getting a life sentence," said Mick.

"Good. The son of a bitch deserves it," said Ethan. He didn't say anything after that.

"We also received word that the assassination attempt on the Prime Minister was orchestrated solely by BMC."

"Jesus...So it was basically a coup?" said Ethan, and Mick slowly nodded.

"It appears that way. BMC wanted to take over the government and install its own leadership," he added. The room fell silent again. Ethan had a TV in his room, and it was showing a news report on the recent terrorist events.

"So...What are you going to do now?" asked Mick. Ethan let out a deep sigh. Then he turned to look at Mick.

"I'm taking a bloody holiday," he said.

"That's a shame...Because I spoke with Anna Mackenzie. She confirmed it with the Commissioner...Are you ready to come back to work?" he asked. Ethan didn't say anything at first. Then he made a cheeky grin.

"I thought you'd never ask," he replied, and Mick just laughed.

TWO YEARS LATER

The Australian Air Force Boeing 787-8 Dreamliner touched down at Canberra Airport. It had just arrived from a quick forty-minute flight from Sydney, carrying the President of Australia, Christine Mills. She had just returned from Sydney after she unveiled a new memorial that was to commemorate those lives lost in the 2020 Independence Day terrorist attack. Christine was driven into the city in a black Range Rover Sports. Christine was still the President of the Republic of Australia. She had served four years in the office of the President, and with one year remaining until her term expires, she wanted to make sure that things would get done. Right now, she was heading over to the Parliament House. She had a meeting with the Prime Minister, something that she had on a regular basis. They were mostly updates about the government agenda and what the government planned to do over the next term.

However, this was to be a different meeting; Christine was informed it was a security meeting. She sat in the back seat of the Range Rover and looked out the window as it drove down Commonwealth Avenue. She was in deep thought and still thinking about the memorial service this morning. Her Official Secretary, Joe Parsons, was sitting in the seat next to her, and he was going over the President's schedule. "How are you feeling, Your Excellency," he said. She looked over from her window. She hesitated before responding.

"I'm okay, Joe. Still thinking about the service," she said, and Joe nodded. "I know. It was a beautiful service though, Ma'am," he said, and Christine made a brief smile.

"Have you got any idea on what this meeting is about?" she asked, but Joe shook his head.

"Not a clue. I got a call from the PM's Chief of Staff. She said it was an urgent meeting," he said. Christine didn't say anything after that. A few moments later, the vehicle pulled into the underground parking garage that was underneath the Parliament House. Christine had a reserved parking space and her vehicle pulled in. A body guard got out and opened the door, allowing Christine to climb out. She smiled, and then she was escorted into the building. Finally, she arrived just outside the Prime Minister's office. Joe Parson's knocked on the door and it opened. The PM's Chief of Staff came out.

"The President is here to see the Prime Minister," said Joe, and she nodded. She showed them in, and Christine and Joe entered. Christine approached the Prime Minister's desk, and she smiled.

"Your Excellency, good to see you this morning," said the Prime Minister, standing up. At the same time, they shook hands.

"Brilliant service today, Your Excellency."

"Thank you, Prime Minister. I was told this was an urgent meeting?" she asked, and the PM nodded.

"Yes. Your Excellency, this is Nick Young, he's a security adviser with ASIO," said the PM. Nick was a young, dashing man wearing a slim tailored suit and a blue tie. "Your Excellency, it's an honour to finally meet you," said Nick. They both shook hands.

"So, what's this about?" asked Christine.

"Ma'am, this information was picked up by our office. It's highly sensitive, so not many people know about it," he said.

"ASIO has determined that there is the possibility of a terrorist attack in Sydney." Christine's eyes widened. She looked at the Prime Minister.

"What sort of attack?" she asked.

"ASIO believes it involves radioactive material," he replied.

"My God…How is this happening?"

"It's unclear, but from what ASIO has released, a terrorist group has or soon will be taking possession of the material," he explained. Christine looked at Joe, shocked by this.

"Does ASIO know who is involved in this?" she asked.

"At this point, they suspect an ISIS cell is behind it," said Nick.

"Unbelievable...What's being done to resolve this?" she asked.

"ASIO is coordinating the investigation with the AFP. The Serious Crimes Unit will be heading up the investigation," Nick replied, and Christine nodded.

"I've made arrangements for the SCU and other agencies so they have access to unlimited resources," the Prime Minister added.

"Very well. Is there anything else you need from me?" asked Christine, as she stood up.

"No, we'll keep you apprised of any updates, Your Excellency," said Nick. She then shook hands with the Prime Minister.

"Thank you, Prime Minister, Mr. Young," said Christine. She then turned and headed towards the door. Joe was following her.

"I can't believe this is happening," she said, as they headed down the corridor.

"I take it that wasn't a good meeting?" he asked.

"No. I just found out that terrorists are planning an attack in Sydney," said Christine. Joe was shocked.

"My God...Who's behind it?"

"They think it's the UAG again…I want to keep an open line of communication with the PM's office," said replied.

"Yes, Your Excellency."

Mick Greer stood by the window of his office. He was still the Chief Inspector of the Serious Crimes Unit. He temporarily took command of the agency, as Chief Superintendent Anna Mackenzie was in Canberra at the AFP headquarters. It was just after eight o'clock in the morning and he was getting himself ready for a long day. He was looking out the window and sipped on his morning coffee. As he stood there day dreaming, there was a knock on the door of his office. Ethan Cooper stepped in. "Morning, Boss," he said.

"Ethan, thanks for coming in. Is everyone here?" he asked.

"Yeah, we're all ready for the briefing. Also, Detective Sergeant Simon Harper is here," Ethan replied. Mick took one last sip of his coffee and placed it down on his desk.

"Yes, of course. Welcome to the Serious Crimes Unit. Ethan's told me all about you," said Mick. They both shook hands.

"All good stuff, I hope," Simon replied, sarcastically, and the three of them started laughing.

"Right, let's get to it," he said. They then headed out the door. Walking together, they made their way across the floor to the agency's briefing room. "So, you two were in the same SASR squad?" asked Mick, as they approached the glass door.

"Yes, that's correct. We were colleagues for ten years," said Simon.

"That's great. This should be a walk in the park for you then," Mick replied. He opened the door and showed them both in. Everyone was there waiting, including Detective Sergeant Samuel Hunter and Felicity Meyers were also in attendance. "Morning all…First things first, a few housekeeping items," said Mick, as he went inside. "I'd like to introduce Detective Sergeant Simon Harper. He's just joined the task force, so please, make him feel welcome." At that, everyone clapped. "Right. Let's get to it…I appreciate you all coming in so early. But we have a situation…I've been informed that we have a potential terrorist threat," he began. Everyone looked at each other.

"Do we know what kind of threat?" asked Ethan Cooper, breaking the silence.

"ASIO believes that it involves radioactive material," he said. "They also suspect the UAG is behind it." The room fell silent after that.

"Bloody hell…I thought the UAG was dismantled after they assassinated the Prime Minister and tried to take out the President?" asked Sam, remembering what happened two years ago.

"They were, but it appears not all cell members were accounted for. The UAG is an extensive network, and BMC did not have all names listed on their registry," said Mick.

"Do we know who's in charge of the cell?" asked Sam Hunter, again. Simon glanced over at Sam.

"ASIO has identified this man..." Mick clicked a button on the remote. An image appeared on the screen of a Caucasian man. He was photographed talking with several people. "We believe the operation is being led by Matthias Granger...He was a mercenary working for BMC and wanted for arms smuggling into East Timor," Mick explained.

"Have we got any leads on potential associates?" asked Ethan. Then Mick pressed another button.

"ASIO has also been watching this man...Stuart Mason," he said. The image changed, and a younger looking man appeared; he would be in his early thirties, very masculine looking with broad shoulders. "It appears Mason has been running things in the field. He too was a mercenary for Birchall McClelland."

"So, what exactly are we dealing with?" asked Simon Harper.

"ASIO sent over this file." Mick pressed a button on his remote. It turned on the TV screen and a satellite image of Sydney appeared. "From what we know, the material that was stolen, is highly enriched uranium...They believe ISIS is attempting to build a radiological dirty bomb," he explained. The room fell silent after that.

"Bloody hell," said Detective Sergeant Samuel Hunter.

"ASIO has analyzed the effects of a dirty bomb if it were to be detonated here in Sydney." Mick pressed another button.

"This represents the detonation of a dirty bomb at ground zero. Ground zero being city hall. Estimated casualties would be between 1,400 and 3,000 people," he said.

"But the real killer is the radiation. With the release of radiation, that number could easily end up in the tens of thousands." No one said a word. They were just in shock.

"How did the terrorists get their hands on such material?" asked Sam.

"That's a good question. Right now, ASIO has learnt that the terrorists acquired the material from the Parramatta District Hospital. Hospital staff reported the theft of radioactive material from their storage containment unit," said Mick. "I'm sending out a team to search the hospital for any leads...In the meantime, Ethan, Sam, I want you two to head over to Goulburn Correctional Center. We need to find out what these guys are up to. Our best source of Intel right now is Karl Benedict," said Mick. Ethan closed his eyes.

"You can't be serious, Mick?" Ethan snapped.

"Ethan, I realize this is going to be difficult for you, but Mackenzie wants us to find out what he knows," said Mick.

"I bet she does. The guy's a psychopath, Boss. The only thing he's going to want is a get-out-of-jail-free card," said Ethan. The room fell silent after that.

"Be that as it may, these are your orders...There's a chopper waiting on the rooftop. Wheels up in five...Let's go." At that, everyone got up and headed out the door to get to work. Ethan started heading to the door, but as he was about to leave, he was stopped. "Ethan, can I have a moment?" asked Mick.

"Sure." Ethan closed the door and went over to take a seat.

"How are you coping?"

"Fine, I'm doing okay. Not looking forward to having to question Benedict again," he added, and Mick nodded.

"I understand, but there's nothing I can do to change it," he said. "Look...I wanted to talk to you alone because we're currently running an undercover operation," said Mick. Ethan's eyes widened.

"I see. Who's the undercover officer?" he asked.

"It's Diane Faulkner. She's currently working undercover with Stuart Mason. She managed to gain his trust and started working with him twelve weeks ago," said Mick.

"These images were taken by an ASIO Intelligence Officer. He's been in contact with Diane Faulkner while she's been undercover."

"Bloody hell...And Mason actually bought her cover?" Mick nodded.

"Yes...She originally approached Mason and posed as a high-class escort. From there, she built a connection with him, and she revealed that she was in fact a corrupt mercenary looking for extra money," said Mick. "What I'm asking is, are you able to take over the case and become Diane's handler?" he asked. "We need to stop these terrorists before they set off this dirty bomb..." the room fell silent after that, and Ethan looked at the screen. He saw an image of Stuart Mason and

Matthias talking with each other. At the same time, Simon Harper was sitting at his desk and he was watching as Ethan and Mick were talking in the briefing room.

"Fine...I'll do it," said Ethan.

Warrick was sick. He sat in the rear passenger seat of the van, hugging his knees, wondering what he had gotten himself into. He had seen some bad shit in prison, but nothing like this. In front of him, Edward was on the phone, shouting something. Most of it was abusive words. Edward had been making calls for hours now. The words didn't mean anything to Warrick. It all sounded like gibberish. The real deal, Edward had trained in London as a chemical engineer, but instead of getting a job, he had gone to war. In his early 30s, a wide scar across one cheek, to hear him tell it, he had waged jihad in half a dozen countries—and had come to Australia to do the same. He screamed into the phone again and again before he got through. When he finally reached someone, he launched into the first of several shouted arguments. After a few minutes, he settled down and listened. Then he hung up. Warrick's face was flushed. He had a fever. He could feel it burning through his body. His heart was racing. He hadn't thrown up, but he felt like he was going to. They had waited at the rendezvous point at Strathfield Train Station, which the half way point to the city, for over two hours. It was supposed to be a simple thing. Steal the materials, drive the van ten minutes, meet the contacts and walk away. But the contacts never showed. Now they were…somewhere.

Warrick didn't know. He had passed out for a while. He was awake again, but everything seemed like a vague dream. They were on the highway. Marcus was driving, so he must know where they were going. A technology expert, Marcus, skinny with no muscle tone, looked the part. He was so young the smooth skin of his face didn't have a single line. "We have new instructions," Edward said. Warrick groaned, wishing he was dead. He didn't know it was possible to feel this sick.

"I have to get out of this van," Warrick said.

"Shut up, Warrick!" All that stuff was in the back of the van. There was a lot of it, in all kinds of canisters and boxes. Some of it had leaked out, and now it was killing them. It had killed Brett already. The dummy had opened a canister when they still were down in the vault. He was immensely strong, and he wrenched the lid off. Why did he do that? Warrick could picture him holding the canister up.

"There's nothing in here," he'd said. Then he'd held it to his nose. Within a minute, he started coughing. He just sort of sank down to his knees. Then he was on all fours, coughing.

"I have something in my lungs," he said. "I can't get it out." He started gasping for air. The sound was horrible. Edward walked up and shot him in the back of the head.

"Believe me, I did him a favour," he'd said. Now, the van was passing through a tunnel. The tunnel was long and narrow and dark, with orange lights zooming by overhead. The lights made Warrick dizzy.

"I have to get out of this van!" he shouted. "I have to get out of this van! I have to..." Edward turned around. His gun was out. He pointed it at Warrick's head.

"Quiet! I'm on the phone." Edward's sliced up face was flushed red. He was sweating.

"You gonna kill me the way you did Brett?"

"Brett was my friend," Edward said. "I killed him out of mercy. I will kill you just to shut you up." He pressed the muzzle of the gun against Warrick's forehead.

"Shoot me. I don't care." Warrick closed his eyes. When he opened them again, Edward had turned back around. They were still in the tunnel. The lights were too much. A sudden wave of nausea passed through Warrick, and a great up-rushing spasm gripped his body. His stomach clenched, and he tasted acid in his throat. He bent over and threw up on the floor between his shoes. A few seconds passed. The stench wafted up into his face, and he wretched again. Oh God, he begged silently. Please let me die.

Wendy Carmichael was a proud mother. Today, her youngest son, Daniel Carmichael was getting married, and it was about time too as she had been waiting for so long for this to happen. Wendy was a mother of two sons; Daniel, being the youngest, and Eric Carmichael was the eldest, but only by two years. The three of them had been through a lot this past year, having suffered the loss of their father. The Carmichael family was one of the wealthiest families in the country; the father, Harry Carmichael, was an iron ore mining magnate. When he passed away, his wife, Wendy, inherited the company and its finances. She lived with her sons at the family mansion in Sydney's Mosman, one of the most expensive suburbs. The mansion was a hidden masterpiece and was built as a Mediterranean villa inspired home.

The Carmichaels had lived there all their lives as their father, Harry Carmichael's Grandfather built it. The mansion boasted elegant views across Sydney Harbour and contained well-manicured gardens as well as a sparkling mosaic pool. Twenty-four-year-old Daniel Carmichael was getting married to a Rana Denali; she was an employee of Carmichael Prospectus and had been living in Australia for ten years. She was a migrant from the Middle-East, but one of the lucky ones. Rana Denali was relaxing by the pool and catching up on some work. She was Wendy Carmichael's Chief Financial Officer and handled all the company's finances.

As she sat there reviewing the company's latest financial reports, a shadow crept up behind her. She jumped and turned around to see that it was only her fiancé, Daniel Carmichael. He smiled and leaned down to give her a kiss. "Sweetheart, you scared me," she said.

"What do you think you're doing?" he said, noticing that she was working. "I'm just checking up on the latest statements," said Rana. Daniel let out a sigh. "Rana, we're getting married in less than twelve hours...It is our wedding day!" he said.

"I know, I'm sorry. I just had to check to see if everything was in order."

"You work too hard...Today is supposed to be our special day," he said. He gave her another kiss.

"I'm sorry, I just couldn't help myself," she replied. Daniel shook his head.

"Well, you can make it up to me by following me into the bedroom," he said, cheekily. Rana grinned with excitement and she quickly got up.

Watching from the window was twenty-six-year-old Eric Carmichael. He stood there with his arms crossed over and watched as his brother consorted with his fiancé. Ever since they got together, Eric was somewhat wary of Rana Denali. There was something about her that he just didn't like. It wasn't out of jealousy, but more of a concerned brother.

He suspected that Rana Denali was involved with terrorism, and secretly, he'd hired a private investigator to look into Rana's background. So far, the investigator hadn't found anything, but he wasn't going to give up that easily. As he stood there, his mobile phone started ringing.

"Hello?" he answered.

"Mr. Carmichael, it's Aaron Morgan." Eric turned away from the window and went to a private area.

"Hey Aaron, what's going on? I didn't expect to hear from you today."

"I know, but something came up and I had to contact you as soon as possible," he said.

"Okay, what's wrong? Does this have something to do with my brother's fiancé?"

"Unfortunately, yes. I've been looking deeper into Rana Denali's background like you requested. I found some irregularities that don't add up."

"What kind of irregularities?" he asked, becoming concerned.

"It appears that Rana Denali has had a connection with an internationally recognized terrorist by the name of Abad Nasir. He was responsible for several terrorist attacks in Germany, and the United Kingdom," said Aaron. The line fell silent. Eric didn't know what to say.

"My God…So, you're saying that Rana Denali knows this Abad Nasir?" he asked.

"It's unclear as to the extent of her connection with Nasir. But in order for us to get a better understanding of Rana's involvement, we need some more personal information," he said.

"Like, what kind of personal information?"

"Ideally, her recent travel entries from her passport would help," he said.

"That's not exactly going to be easy to get a hold of. I don't even know where she keeps her passport," said Eric.

"I know this is a lot to ask, but if you want us to find out what her connection is to Abad Nasir, this is the way we're going to do it," said Aaron. Eric just let out a sigh.

"Just how will this help with the investigation?" he asked.

"It will help us to find out where she's travelled over the past twelve months, and get a more detailed background check," said Aaron. Eric closed his eyes. He paused for a moment and let out a deep breath.

"Okay, fine. I'll see what I can do," he replied.

"Good. I'm sorry to have to ask you to do this, Eric. But it's the only way we're going to get anywhere with this investigation."

"I know...I'll do it."

"Thanks. Call me when you have those entries." Eric hung up the phone and stood there feeling a bit overwhelmed. He had no idea how he was going to do this, but he had to. He wanted to make sure that his brother wasn't marrying a terrorist.

It was a busy day ahead for Christine Mills, the President of Australia. On top of being the head of state, she was thrust into a crisis. She couldn't believe that terrorists were planning to detonate a radiological dirty bomb in Sydney. She was currently in her office at the Government House in Canberra and reviewing an official report from ASIO; it was stating the effects of what would happen if the bomb detonated and the amount of people that'd be affected by it. The TV was on and it was showing a news report on the PM's recent parliament address regarding his new security measures to help combat terrorism. As the President sat there reading the report, there was a knock at the door. Her Official Secretary, Joe Parsons entered. "Ah, Joe. Come in. I've just been reviewing the latest report from ASIO," she said.

"Yes, I've just read it myself."

"I can't believe the damage this device would cause if it's detonated," said Christine.

"I know, it's devastating. But we will find it before that happens," said Joe. The room fell silent after that. Christine went back to reading, and she took a sip of her coffee. "Have you ah, spoken with John recently?" he asked, changing the subject. Christine didn't reply straight away.

"Not since yesterday. He's in Perth at the moment. He's giving a speech at a fundraiser," she replied.

"Well, that's good…By the way, I know this probably isn't the best time, but, I wanted to talk to you about the list," said Joe. Christine rolled her eyes.

"Really, Joe. Do you think it's such a good idea to be even talking about who my predecessor is going to be, especially when we're facing a crisis," she said.

"I realise that, Ma'am, but your term is up in the next eighteen months, and the APSC are requesting your choice," said Joe.

The APSC was the Australian Presidential Selection Committee; it was a committee formed after the republic referendum was passed and consisted of members of the Australian government to interview, select and nominate a candidate to be appointed to the office of the President of Australia. Even though Christine still had eighteen months left in office, she was required to submit her recommendation of candidates to be shortlisted. The list of course was also to be approved by the Prime Minister. Christine let out a sigh and rolled her eyes.

"Alright, fine. Who's first to be interviewed?" she asked.

"New South Wales Governor Brendan King is flying in this morning. You'll meet with him at ten o'clock," said Joe, and Christine nodded. She took a sip of her coffee and went back to reading her report.

Eric Carmichael was still a bit unsure about what he had to do. He was being asked to steal personal information about his brother's fiancé without her knowing. But, it was the only way he was going to find out if Rana Denali was working for terrorists. He was in the kitchen drinking a cup of coffee. He still had no idea how he was going to get the passport from Rana. He stood there drinking his coffee, when suddenly, he almost spilt it as he was scared by his brother, Daniel, who just came wandering in. He was buttoning up his white frilled shirt. "Hey bro, is that coffee?" he said, pointing at the cup.

"Jesus Danny, you scared the crap out of me," he said, while cleaning himself. "Yeah, it's coffee, why?"

"We need something a bit stronger than that. It's my wedding day!" he said, with excitement. Daniel was somewhat a party animal and found any excuse to have a drink. He inherited the habit from his father, who was a chronic alcoholic.

"Don't you think it's a bit early for that?" asked Eric, as he watched Daniel open a bottle of beer.

"It's never too early for a beer, especially when you're getting married," he said. He looked at Eric oddly. "Bro, you look so tense, what's up?" he asked. Eric immediately dismissed him.

"No, I'm fine. Just needed this," he said, indicating to the coffee. "By the way, where's Rana?" he asked, changing the subject.

"She's upstairs, getting ready. Why?" Eric didn't reply straight away.

"No reason, just thought I'd see if she wanted something to drink," he said. Daniel just stared at him, strangely.

"Okay, well I'm going to see if they need help setting up outside. Later," he said, and he wandered off outside with his beer. Eric watched him leave. He thought this would be his ideal moment. He made his way out of the kitchen and headed up the flight of stairs. There were three bedrooms upstairs; one was his mother's, the other belonged to Rana and Daniel, and the third was a study. Eric's bedroom was downstairs. He walked passed his mother's bedroom and saw that she was on the phone talking with an employee at the office. He went down the hallway and approached Daniel and Rana's room. The door was slightly ajar and as he got closer, he could hear that the shower was on. His heart was racing the whole time, as he'd never done anything like this before. Carefully, he pushed the door open. There was no sign of Rana, so she must have been in the shower. He went into the bedroom, and quietly walked over to the dresser. It was covered with Rana's makeup and beauty stuff. Eric started opening the draws, quietly of course, and checked each of them to see if her passport was there. Several of the draws came up empty; he started to panic. Then, he opened one of the draws and saw on the top, a leather case. He thought for a moment and then picked it up. Unzipping it, he found several documents and letters. One of the documents was her passport. He couldn't believe it. He picked it up and started flicking through the pages. He found the one that contained all the countries she'd visited – there were quite a few so he had to be quick – he began to write them down on a scrap piece of paper. As he got through half of them, he heard the shower turn off. He knew he was running out of time, so he kept writing, quicker. Finally, he got the last one written down, and then put the passport back and shoved the case back in the draw.

He got up and snuck out the door. His heart was still racing as he headed down the hallway. But at the same time, he felt proud of himself for getting it done. As he headed down the stairs, he took out his mobile phone and dialled a number. It rang a few times, but someone finally picked up.

"Aaron Morgan."

"Hey Aaron, it's Eric. I got that passport information you asked for," he said.

"That's great. Why don't you send those over, and I'll get started?"

"Okay, I'll just take a photo." He then grabbed the piece of paper and took a picture of the information. Within a couple of seconds, the photo was sent through. "Did you get it?" he asked.

"Yeah, I just got it then. I'll cross reference this information with the Department of Immigration and Border Protection to see if we get any inconsistencies," said Aaron.

"So, how long is this going to take?"

"I should get something in an hour, so I'll give you a call back," he said. Eric let out a sigh.

"Alright, thanks Aaron." Eric hung up the phone.

There was a lot of activity going on at the Parliament House in Canberra. Allen Brady had been in his office since the early hours of the morning dealing with the crisis. David Pritchard, the Chief of Staff to the Prime Minister, made his way down the corridor. He turned the corner and approached the main entrance way to the PM's office. He was greeted by the Prime Minister's executive secretary, and she got up to go to the door. David was shown into the office, and the Prime

Minister was sitting at his desk. He was currently on the phone with the AFP Commissioner. "Yes, thank you for the update Commissioner. We'll talk soon," he said, and hung up. He looked up at David who approached him. David was accompanied by Nick Young. Nick was a short man of about five foot three, with circular spectacles and wore a buttoned shirt with a black vest. "Ah, David. Come in. What's the latest?" he asked, as the door closed.

"Prime Minister, Nick Young is here with an update on the missing nuclear material," said David.

"That's good. Has there been any progress on that?"

"Not yet, Sir. I've been keeping in contact with the SCU in Sydney," said David, and the PM nodded. "Nick Young is here to give you a breakdown on what's likely to happen if such a disaster were to take place," he added.

"Of course, what have you got, Mr. Young?" Nick stepped forward. He held a Smart tablet in his hand, which were all slippery from him sweating so much. Nick was nervous, considering he was standing in front of the Prime Minister.

"Prime Minister, thank you for seeing me again. I've received some Intel from ANSTO which outlines what exactly is a dirty bomb, and its effects," said Nick.

"I see…Let's hear it," said the PM.

"From what ANSTO has told us, a "dirty bomb" is one type of a radiological dispersal device, also called an RDD, that combines conventional explosives, such as dynamite, with radioactive material. Most RDDs would not release enough radiation to kill people or cause severe illness. The conventional explosive itself would be more harmful to individuals than the radioactive material. However, depending on the situation, an RDD explosion could create fear and panic, contaminate property, and require potentially costly clean-up. Making prompt, accurate information available to the public may prevent the panic sought by the terrorists," Nick explained as he read the information from his tablet. He scrolled down further, and continued, "a dirty bomb is in no way similar to a nuclear weapon or nuclear bomb. A nuclear bomb creates an explosion that is millions of times more powerful than that of a dirty bomb. The cloud of radiation from a nuclear bomb could spread tens to hundreds of square miles, whereas a dirty bomb's radiation could be dispersed within a few blocks or miles of the explosion. A dirty bomb is not a "Weapon of Mass Destruction" but a "Weapon of Mass Disruption," where contamination and anxiety are the terrorists' major objectives," he said. There was a sudden pause of silence in the room, as the PM looked at David, shocked.

"I can't believe this," said the PM, shaking his head.

"Shall I continue, Prime Minister?" asked Nick.

"Yes of course, carry on, Mr. Young."

"The extent of local contamination would depend on a number of factors, including the size of the explosive, the amount and type of radioactive material used, the means of dispersal, and weather conditions. Those closest to the RDD would be the most likely to sustain injuries due to the explosion. As radioactive material spreads, it becomes less concentrated and less harmful. Prompt detection of the type of radioactive material used will greatly assist local authorities in advising the community on protective measures, such as sheltering in place, or quickly leaving the immediate area. Radiation can be readily detected with equipment already carried by many emergency responders. Subsequent decontamination of the affected area may involve considerable time and expense," said David, and Madelaine nodded. The look of sheer horror on the Prime Minister's face showed Nick and David just how serious this situation was.

"My God…If this device is set off, we could be looking at mass panic throughout Sydney," said the Prime Minister, and Nick nodded. "David, I want you to make sure that the SCU and AFP have all the necessary resources available. Make sure they stop this from happening," he added.

"Of course. I'm coordinating with the Chief Superintendent of the SCU," said David.

"Thanks David, Mr. Young. Keep me updated," said the Prime Minister. They both nodded and then headed to the door.

Detective Sergeant Ethan Cooper was not looking forward to this meeting at all. He never expect to be coming face to face with the nation's most sinister criminal mastermind. He was about to meet for the first time in two years, Karl

Benedict, who had been residing in Goulburn Correctional Centre for all that time. Ethan Cooper sat in the main cabin of the black Bell 408 helicopter. The helicopter was charted as a courtesy to the Serious Crimes Unit. They were in a hurry, and what would normally take them a two hour drive, they got here in less than forty minutes. The chopper gently touched down in a nearby field several hundred metres away from Goulburn Correctional Centre. Both Ethan and Sam climbed out of the chopper and made their way over to the main entrance of the prison. Upon entering the prison, they underwent security checks. During which, they were asked to relinquish their hand guns, as weapons were not permitted inside the prison. Once they cleared security, they were shown in and were met by the prison's chief correctional officer. "Good morning. You must be the detectives from the city?" asked the officer.

"Yes, that's correct. Detectives Ethan Cooper, Sam Hunter. We're with the Serious Crimes Unit," said Ethan. They began walking down a long corridor, its windows barred.

"I understand you're here to interview one of the inmates?"

"That's correct. We're here to question Karl Benedict...We believe he has Intel on a terrorist threat that has the potential to threaten tens of thousands of lives," Ethan explained.

"I see. The prisoner is being transferred to one of our interview rooms. Once inside the room, you will be accompanied by two prison guards," said the officer. Ethan and Sam followed him further down the corridor. They were then led into a small room. There was a double-sided mirror on the wall and looked directly into the interview room; it was very similar to one of the SCU's holding rooms. They stood there and waited for a moment, when a door opened. At that, Karl Benedict was hauled into the room. He was dressed in light grey prison overalls, and his hair was shaved right back. It looked as though prison life had been quite hard on him over the past two years. Karl Benedict was seated at the table. His hands hand cuffed to the centre of it. The two prison guards stepped back and took up their positions. "Okay, he's ready for you," said the officer, indicating to the door. Ethan's heart was racing the whole time. He had no idea how he was going to feel after seeing this son of a bitch again. He and Sam headed to the door and it was unlocked. When he stepped in, Karl looked up. A cheesy grin appeared on his face.

"Well, well…Ethan Cooper," he said. Of course, Ethan didn't say anything at first. "I never expected to be seeing you again." Ethan came up to the table and sat down. He placed a folder in front of him and opened it. "You know, I've thought about you every single day I've been in this place for the past two years," said Karl. "I have to say, I admire your strength to come see me."

"This isn't a social call, Benedict," said Sam, abruptly.

"And of course, Detective Constable Sam Hunter."

"It's Detective Sergeant, now," Sam replied, bitterly. The room fell silent for a moment.

"We're here because the SCU believes you can help with a national security threat," said Ethan.

"I doubt I'd be much help to the SCU. You're forgetting where I've been living for the past two years, Cooper," said Karl.

"I'm sure you'd be able to come up with something...We have Intel that the UAG is plotting to detonate a radiological dirty bomb in Sydney," said Ethan. "Tens of thousands of lives are at stake, Benedict. We need to stop these bastards before they carry out their threat." Karl just sat there, grinning.

"Interesting...And what makes you think I'll be willing to help you?"

"Because, we can offer you a reduced sentence. You give us what you know, and I'll help you out with better accommodation," said Ethan. Karl paused, and he was contemplating the offer.

"How much does the SCU know already?" he asked.

"We know that the UAG have possession of uranium U-235...We also know that the man behind this threat, is a man named Matthias Granger," said Ethan.

"That's troubling...Matthias was one of my best men. He used to operate an arms dealing scheme in East Timor," said Karl.

"Yes, we're aware of his operations...Why is he doing this?" asked Sam.

"After the downfall of my company, most of my operatives went dark. They weren't happy that they lost their source of income," said Karl.

"What does that have to do with Matthias?"

"I don't know, but whatever happened, he's obviously gone insane," said Karl.

"So, you're saying that Matthias is operating on his own accord?"

"It looks like it. I'm afraid I can't help you any further, Detective Cooper," said Karl. Ethan just sat there, staring at Karl, looking rather frustrated.

Ever since the assassination attempt in 2021, the Universal Adversary Group had been dismantled. All terrorist members of the group were apprehended and were either killed or imprisoned. Matthias Granger was the leader of the terrorist cell in Sydney. He was a mercenary and used to work for Birchall McClelland. Today, he along with a group of dedicated men, were planning to carry out an attack that would bring the government to its knees. Matthias wanted to bring down the government because of what it did to Birchall McClelland. The group was hiding out in an abandoned warehouse at the Sydney Carriage-works tram sheds. Matthias had purchased the warehouse using his own money and thought it was the ideal location, as it was within proximity to the city. At the far end of the warehouse,

Matthias Granger had a large workstation set up for him to work and check up on his men. He wore a classy business suit and tie and his hair gelled back with a barber style cut.

He sat at his desk and checked his emails. Matthias Granger sat there and caught up with the latest news regarding politics. As he sat there, his Blackberry phone started ringing. "Yes?" he answered.

"It's me. We're at the location." The voice also replied.

"Have you got the scientist yet?" he asked.

"Not yet. He's scheduled to leave any moment now," said a voice on the other end.

"Good. Edward and Marcus will be returning with the material soon," said Matthias, checking his expensive looking wrist watch.

"No problem. We'll have the target shortly," said the voice, and then the call hung up. Matthias put his phone down and grinned. Then he went back to watching the news.

Dr. Marc Cameron was a Professor at the University of Sydney. He was an expert in the field of Physics. He'd been teaching for the last ten years, but also worked at the Australian Nuclear Science and Technology Organisation as a research scientist in nuclear medicine; he also had a Master's degree in engineering. Marc was currently giving a lecture on physics to a lecture theatre full of eager students. It was approaching exam time and he had quite a bit of work to do. "And so, to conclude, I can only emphasize enough to make sure that you all do twice as much research as you've done previously. It's important that you all do as much revision as possible before the exam. Also, assignment number four is due by the end of next week," he said. "If any of you have questions or queries about the assignment, or need help with it, you know where my office is," he added, "alright, that's all we have time for today. You can find all the lecture materials online, and of course, if you need further assistance, come see me during my consultation times, thank you," he finished. Then, everyone started getting up and began piling out the door. As they began to leave, Marc started packing up his books and other material into his briefcase. Afterwards, he made his way out of the building as he'd just finished his last lecture for the day.

He walked over to the staff carpark and unlocked the door of his silver BMW. About five hundred metres away, there was a dark coloured van parked. Stuart Mason and Kelly Duncan sat in the front of the van and watched their target, Marc Cameron.

"So, that's him?" asked Kelly, as they saw him putting his stuff in the back seat.

"That's our boy. Granger wants this done as soon as possible," said Mason. Kelly Duncan was SCU Detective Sergeant Diane Faulkner, as she was an undercover agent. She'd been working undercover with Mason for the past twelve weeks in an attempt to locate the leader of the cell, Matthias Granger. Mason used to be a mercenary for Birchall

McClelland, one of their best. However, after the company was disbanded, Mason, along with many other of its employees, had disappeared. Mason was hired by Matthias to do an important job. "Okay, let's do this," he said. He started up the van, and quickly put his foot down on the accelerator. The van came to a screeching halt and stopped right next to Marc's car.

He was shocked as to what was going on. The van's sliding door opened, and several other men got out wearing balaclavas. They immediately grabbed hold of Marc and knocked him unconscious using a cloth soaked in chloroform. Then, he was dragged over and dumped into the van. At that, the van quickly sped off in the opposite direction. As it drove, Mason got out his phone to dial a number. "It's me...We've got the scientist," he said. "Copy that. We'll be there in ten." He hung up and looked over at Kelly Duncan. "Looks like it's your lucky day. We're going to see the Boss," he added. Diane's heart started pounding, as this was to be the first time she'd be meeting Matthias Granger.

Eric Carmichael was still a bit overwhelmed by the fact that he was forced to steal personal information from his brother's fiancé. He didn't feel comfortable at all doing it, but it was the only way he could help his brother. The annoying thing now was the waiting game. He was waiting for a call back from his private investigator, Aaron Morgan. Eric was making himself a drink as his nerves were shot to pieces. As he took a sip, he jumped when his mother, Wendy Carmichael came in. "Sweetie, are you okay?" she asked.

"Yeah, sorry Mum. You just startled me," he replied.

"Are you sure you're okay? You just seem on edge," said Wendy, resting her hand on his shoulder.

"Honestly, I'm fine. Just think it's the fact that my younger brother is getting married in a few hours," he said. She didn't know what to say to that.

"Look, I know you miss your father, today of all days. But we need to be supportive of Danny. He's getting married," said Wendy, with a smile. Eric didn't say anything at first, and took a sip of his drink. Just then, his mobile started ringing.

"Sorry Mum, I've got to take this," he said. He answered the call, and started walking away. "Hello?"

"Eric, it's Aaron Morgan. Are you alone?" he asked.

"Yeah, what's the verdict?" There was a slight pause.

"I'm not going to sugar-coat it, because it's not good...From the passport information you gave us, we've confirmed that Rana Denali has had contact with Abad Nasir," said Aaron. Eric's heart sank. He couldn't believe what he was hearing.

"So, what you're saying is...Rana Denali is a terrorist?"

"I'm afraid it looks that way...And because of this new information, I've had to report it to ASIO, as well as the AFP," said Aaron.

"My God...What does that mean, are they going to arrest Rana?"

"Possibly, but they'll most likely question her first. It's important for you to not discuss this with any one until she's been questioned," said Aaron.

"You can't expect me to not say anything to anyone."

"No, the last thing I want you to do is to tip her off that she's being investigated. If she is working for this, Abad Nasir, it might trigger an attack," he said. Eric didn't reply to that. His heart was pounding.

"Okay, fine. How long will it be before the AFP get here?" he asked. "I've already sent off the information packet to ASIO. They'll review it and then pass it on to the AFP," he explained.

"It will probably be within half an hour."

"I can't believe this is happening," he said.

"I know, and I am sorry about this. Just try to remain calm," said Aaron.

"How can I remain calm? I just found out that my brother's fiancé is a terrorist," he said.

"I didn't mean it like that, I'm just trying to help you, Eric," he said.

"I know, I'm sorry…Thank you for your help, Aaron."

"We'll talk later." Then the call disconnected.

"Who was that?" asked Wendy Carmichael. Eric spun around quickly, almost dropping his phone.

"Oh, it was no one important."

"Don't give me that, who was it? Sounded important," she replied. Eric closed his eyes.

"Fine, you'll find out sooner or later anyway." She looked at him confused.

"Find out what?" He walked up to her and took his mother's hand. "Sweetheart, what's going on? You're scaring me."

"There's something I've been meaning to tell you. It's about Rana Denali," he said.

"What about her?"

"I've been looking into Rana's activities over the past couple of months, and noticed some inconsistencies is the company's books...At first I thought it was just a computer error, but then it kept happening. So, I decided to look further...I hired a private investigator to look into Rana's activities. It turns out that the private investigator found something bad...She's been in contact with a known terrorist," he explained. Wendy just looked at him, with shock. Her eyes widened, and she gasped in disbelief.

"Do you realise how insane that sounds?" she said. "Hiring a private investigator is one thing but suspecting Rana Denali is a terrorist is completely different!" she said.

"I didn't want to believe it either, Mum. But the fact is, the private investigator found out that Rana has been in contact with a wanted terrorist. She's been financing him for the last twelve months," said Eric. Wendy didn't say anything. She started pacing the room in frustration.

"How accurate is this information?"

"It's been confirmed. The private investigator sent it off to ASIO. They're reviewing the information as we speak," said Eric. "Mum, Rana Denali has been lying to us...She's a terrorist."

"Stop saying that, Eric!" Wendy shouted, and she started getting upset. "Rana has been part of this family for the past five years. I hardly believe she's a terrorist!"

"I can't help what the private investigator found…And think about it, she's from the Middle-East." Wendy rolled her eyes.

"Oh, come on, Eric. I raised you better than that!" she snapped. They fell silent after that.

"Look, I'm sorry about this. But I just didn't trust Rana from the moment I met her, and now I know why," he said.

"Well…I have no idea what to say to that," she added.

"You don't have to say anything…It's already done. The AFP will be here within the next hour to question Rana," he said. Wendy just gave him an odd look.

There was a lot going through Christine Mills' mind. For starters, she couldn't get over the fact that terrorists were attempting to detonate a dirty bomb in Sydney, and that if they were successful, tens of thousands of Australians would lose their lives. She was determined to make sure that it didn't happen. Right now, she was in her private study at Government House. She sat at her finely crafted and polished mahogany desk and attempted to sign some letters. However, she was getting frustrated, because every time she went to write, her hand would begin to shake. About three years ago, Christine was diagnosed with Parkinson's Disease; an unfortunate thing to happen, and since she became ill, she'd been fighting to keep it secret.

No one else knew of her illness, apart from her husband, John Taylor, and her Official Secretary, Joe Parsons. When she was approached by the Australian Presidential Selection Committee four years ago, she failed to disclose the fact that she had an impairment and chose to lie to the committee in order to be selected to become President of Australia. She didn't like the fact that she lied, but she knew if she told them, they'd reject her selection.

From that day on, she'd been trying to keep it a secret, which had proven to be a difficult challenge, considering she was such a public figure. She was frustrated by this disease, as it often hit her when she was unexpecting it. As she sat there observing the screen, there was a knock at the door. She didn't even look up as Joe Parsons entered. "Christine, we need to talk," he said. Christine suddenly looked up at him. He never usually called her by her first name, unless there was something wrong.

"What is it, Joe?" she asked, muting the TV, and removing her half-moon shaped glasses.

"I just had a very disturbing phone call," he said. "It seems that someone inside this office knows about your 'condition'," he said. Christine's eyes lit up with fear.

"Are you serious? How the hell did that happen?" she demanded.

"I don't know. But apparently, a freelance journalist got a hold of some convincing evidence that proves you were diagnosed with Parkinson's before your official appointment to the Presidency," he explained. The room fell silent after that. She just lowered her head in disappointment.

"A journalist…Do we know who?" Joe slowly nodded. "Jeremy Stewart, he's one of the country's most talented and recognizable journalists. If he breaks this story, there's no way we'd recover," he said. Christine didn't know what to say to that.

"Unbelievable…We can't let that sleaze ball publish the story, not today at least," she said.

"I agree, but he's a journalist, he's not going to be easy to be persuaded to sit on it," said Joe. Christine thought for a moment. You want me to meet with him, see if I can get him to hold off?" he asked. Christine let out a sigh.

"Give it your best shot," she said. Joe nodded and then headed to the door. Christine just sat there, speechless.

Diane Faulkner was starting to get nervous. She couldn't believe that she was on her way to meet Matthias Granger. She'd been waiting for the past twelve weeks to meet him and she also knew it was going to be a huge risk. She sat in the front passenger seat of the Transit van. Stuart Mason was driving, and he began to slow down as they entered the Carriage-works tram sheds. They drove down a concrete road and finally arrived at their destination. The van went through a plastic sheet that covered the entrance way and pulled up next to several containers. About half a dozen of Matthias Granger's men surrounded the van and were bearing assault rifles. Both Stuart Mason and Diane Faulkner got out. As they did so, the sliding door opened and a couple more men got out. They were dragging the still unconscious Marc Cameron. They dragged him across the floor towards Matthias' desk. He was then dumped into a chair. Matthias was there waiting for them. "So, this is the scientist?" he asked, as Mason and Diane walked up to him.

"Yeah, we got him without any hassles," said Mason. Matthias didn't say anything. He then looked over at Diane.

"And this is?"

"Oh, this is Kelly Duncan. She's a recruit, but eager to the cause," said Mason. Matthias was somewhat apprehensive about Diane being there, it was mostly because she was Caucasian, and the fact that she was a woman.

"Of course, Mr. Mason has mentioned you…Welcome to the team," he said, and Diane smiled. Her heart was racing quite rapidly now.

"Thank you, Sir." Matthias just nodded.

"So, has the material arrived?" asked Mason, changing the subject. Diane could understand some of what they were saying.

"Yes. Edward and Marcus just turned up. Everything is on schedule," said Matthias, becoming pleased. "Wake him up." One of Granger's men went over to Marc and forced him to wake up. He started coughing and splattering.

"What…What's going on?" he said, with a shaky voice.

"Hello, Dr. Cameron. Glad you could join us," said Matthias.

"W-Who are you people? What do you want from me?" Matthias just grinned.

"So many questions…We want you to help us with a project," said Matthias. He then clicked his fingers. Several men came in and were pushing a trolley. It had a large metallic container on it with a yellow radioactive hazard sign on either side. "I'm sure you're aware of what this material is…It's highly enriched uranium U235," he said. "What I want from you is to help us build a radiological dirty bomb using this material." Marc's eyes widened.

"You're insane…Do you know how many people this type of bomb would kill?" he said. Matthias grinned.

"That's the point…Now, if you do this task for us, no harm will come to you or your family," said Matthias.

"You wouldn't dare hurt my family," he said, with a quiver. Matthias paused. He then took a Smartphone from one of his men. He showed Marc the screen and his eyes widened. It was a video showing Marc's wife who was currently walking the kids and playing with them in the local park.

"I only have to say the word, Dr. Cameron…If you want to protect your family, you will help us build this bomb," he said. Marc just stared at Matthias with tears in his eyes.

"Okay…I'll do it…Just don't hurt my family," he sobbed.

"That's what I like to hear," said Matthias, and patted him on the shoulder.

"Matthias!" Mason called out to him. He stood up and walked over to where he was standing.

"What is it?"

"The bomb is ready," he said. Then, several of Matthias' men came over. They were pushing a trolley towards him. On top of the trolley was a large rectangular shaped box.

"Good. I'm trusting you with this next stage in the operation," said Matthias. Mason nodded. Diane was confused as to what was going on.

"What's happening?" she asked, bravely. Both Matthias and Mason looked over at her.

"We're carrying out another attack…This time, it will show these government pricks just how serious we are," said Matthias. Diane started to get worried.

"What's the target?" Matthias didn't reply straight away. He paused as he turned away.

"The Sydney Harbour Bridge." Diane's eyes widened in shock.

The Serious Crimes Unit was on high alert. Chief Inspector Mick Greer had been in his office for the past five minutes on a video conference call with the AFP Commissioner, as well as Anna Mackenzie, since she was in Canberra. He came out of the office and walked over to where Ethan and the others were working. "Ethan, how did it go with Benedict?" asked Mick.

"He didn't know much more than what we already knew. Apparently, Matthias Granger is acting on his own. Benedict told me he's mentally unstable," said Ethan.

"So, a mentally unstable mercenary is in possession of weapons-grade nuclear material and is threatening to use it as a dirty bomb?" said Mick.

"It seems that way, Boss," Ethan replied. The conversation fell silent after that.

"That's disconcerting...I've just got out of a conference call with the Commissioner...We've got a potential lead on the terrorists," he said, "a senior lecturer by the name of Dr. Marc Cameron was kidnapped less than half an hour ago from the carpark at the University of Sydney," he added.

"Jesus...Who's Dr. Cameron?" asked Sam Hunter.

"He's got a background in nuclear physics and worked as a research scientist at ANSTO. We believe he was kidnapped because of his expertise in nuclear science, and fear that he has the capability of constructing a nuclear weapon," he explained.

"Bloody hell...Are there any witnesses to the abduction?" asked Simon Harper.

"As a matter of a fact, yes...We got lucky. The University of Sydney's on-campus CCTV captured the whole thing...Felicity, want to bring it up for us?" he asked. Felicity typed at her computer. A few moments later, video footage appeared on the main screen. It showed several men jumping out of a van and attacking Dr. Marc Cameron. They saw him being shoved into the van and driving off. "Unfortunately, we were unable to get the number plates of the van...However, another lead has developed...It appears that there's a wealthy family in Mosman. It's the Carmichael family, they live on Belmont Road," he said.

"What's their connection to all of this?" asked Simon.

"It appears that one of the family members is marrying a Middle-Eastern woman who has a connection to a wanted terrorist, Abad Nasir," he said. "Now, it may or may not help us with this investigation, but it needs to be followed up…Ethan, Sam, I want you two to go over to the address and question the subject. Felicity will forward you the details," he said.

"No problem, we're on our way," said Ethan. He and Sam got up and headed to the elevator. At the same time, Simon watched as Ethan and Sam walked off.

Joe Parsons took a private jet to Sydney. Since he was a government employee and worked for the President of Australia, he had access to a range of private transport, making it easier for him to conduct the day to day business. After landing at Sydney Airport, he drove a government vehicle into the city. He had scheduled a meeting with Jeremy Stewart, which he was surprised by considering he was such a busy man. Jeremy Stewart had his own studio in the city, where he conducted his journalistic profession. He had about six people working for him, all who had their own jobs to do, from writing, editing and photography. There even a reception desk for scheduling appointments and meetings with Jeremy. Joe pulled up outside the studio building. He went inside through the glass doors and approached the reception desk, where he was greeted by a lovely red-headed receptionist. She smiled as Joe walked up to her. "Good morning, Sir. Can I help you?" she asked.

"Yes, I have an appointment with Jeremy Stewart? Joe Parsons, the President's Official Secretary," he said. The receptionist scanned through her records using the bright red false nail attached to her finger.

"Ah yes, Mr. Stewart is running a bit late, would you mind taking a seat? I'll let him know you're here," she said, and Joe nodded. He then turned and went over to the couches. He slumped down into it and made himself comfortable. He sat there for a few moments, and then was interrupted as Jeremy Stewart came out. He was dressed in a business suit and had short black combed hair.

"Joe, sorry to keep you waiting, buddy. It's been a bit hectic around here the last twenty-four-hours," he said, Joe stood up and they shook hands.

"I can understand that. How's things?"

"Great, it's been a hectic week...I guess this isn't a social call?"

"No, it's not...I came because of something else. The conversation we had earlier, about the President's condition."

"I see. I hope you realize this is a major front-page story. If I publish that story, it's going to win me the Pulitzer Prize without any competition," said Jeremy.

"And you'll be destroying the Presidency in the process."

"Look, someone from inside your office came to me with some pretty convincing evidence stating the President of Australia lied to the people who supported her and loved her. I'd say that deserves justice," said Jeremy. Of course, Joe didn't know what to say.

"I'm not asking you to give up on the story, I'm simply asking you to sit on it for at least another day…Please, Jeremy. For the country's sake." Jeremy let out a sigh. He then looked at his silver Rolex watch.

"Alright, I'll do you a deal…I go live at six o'clock this evening. I'll hold off on publishing the story until then," he said. Joe rolled his eyes.

"That's not good enough, Jeremy. I need you to hold off until tomorrow."

"No, you want more time to figure out a way to get out of facing the truth…But one way or another, this story will see the light," he said, getting up.

"Looks like you might need to start updating your resume by the end of the day," he added, sarcastically. Joe didn't say anything. He just sat there and watched as Jeremy left. He couldn't believe what was happening. He thought for a moment and then headed outside. As he went over to his car, he took out his mobile phone to dial a number.

"President Mills, please. It's Joe Parsons," he said. His call was then transferred.

"Joe, what's happening? Did you meet with Jeremy?"

"Yes, I did. But I'm afraid it was a waste of time. He's not going to sit on the story. He's going live with the story this evening," said Joe. All he could hear on the other end was a frustrating sigh from Christine.

"Unbelievable...We can't let him publish the story, Joe. There must be something we can do to stop him," she said. Joe got into the front seat and thought for a moment.

"There might be a way...Give me a bit of time, I'll get back to you," he said, and then hung up.

Detectives Ethan Cooper and Sam Hunter arrived at the Carmichael family's executive mansion on Belmont Road, in Mosman. Sam was impressed by the sheer elegance of the mansion as he'd never seen anything quite like it. They pulled up outside the main entrance in their sleek black AFP Range Rover Evoque and got out. Together, they walked over to the front door. "I feel a bit under dressed," said Sam, with sarcasm. Ethan just chuckled. Sam rang the doorbell. They waited for a few moments and then someone finally answered. It opened, and Wendy Carmichael answered the door.

"Can I help you?" she asked.

"Yes Ma'am. I'm Detective Sergeant Sam Hunter, this is my partner, Detective Sergeant Cooper. We're with the Serious Crimes Unit, AFP. We'd like to speak with Rana Denali. Does she live here?" asked Sam. They both showed her their AFP badges.

"Yes, she does. What's this about?"

"I'm afraid it's a matter of national security. We need to question her regarding an urgent matter," said Sam.

"Do you have a warrant to question her?"

"As a matter of fact, we do." Ethan handed Sam the warrant and he showed it to Wendy. She looked over it with her half-moon shaped spectacles.

"Very well...Come this way," she said, and showed them in. Wendy led them inside the mansion and showed them into the massive dining room.

"If you'd like to wait here, I'll get Ms. Denali," she said. She closed the door and started to panic.

"Who was at the door?" asked Eric Carmichael.

"The bloody AFP," she said, getting flustered. Eric's eyes widened. "Where's Rana?"

"I think she's in the kitchen sorting out lunch," said Wendy.

"Go and get her and make sure your brother doesn't see this." Eric scurried off to the kitchen. Rana was there and was helping the kitchen staff get lunch ready.

"Hey Eric. I haven't seen you all morning," she said. Eric smiled. "What's up?"

"Ah, there's a couple of detectives here, from the AFP. They want to talk to you," he said. Rana stopped working, and her eyes widened.

"Talk to me about what?" she insisted.

"It's a matter of national security. That's all they said." Rana didn't reply straight away, and she walked over to him, not looking impressed.

"Eric, what the hell is this about?" she demanded.

"I don't know any more than that," he said.

"They're in the dining room." Rana gave him an odd look and started walking out. As she walked over to the dining room, Wendy Carmichael was standing there.

"Wendy, what's going on? Why does the AFP want to speak with me?" she asked.

"I don't know, Rana. Just go in and talk to them. I'll be waiting out here," she said. Rana paused. Then, she opened the door and went in. Ethan and Sam were sitting at the table and got up as she entered.

"Who are you?"

"Ma'am, we're Detectives Cooper and Hunter, Australian Federal Police. We'd like to ask you a couple of questions regarding your connection to a terrorist group," said Sam. Rana just looked at them, shocked.

"Excuse me?" she said. "I have no idea what you're talking about," she replied.

"Ms. Denali…We have financial records that indicate you've been supporting a known terrorist by the name of Abad Nasir," said Sam.

"I don't understand, what records?"

"Why don't you take a seat, Ms. Denali?" said Ethan. She looked at him, sharply. She paused for a moment and then went over to sit down. Sam showed her a computer file and had detailed financial records from Rana Denali's bank account. She couldn't believe what she was seeing.

"There must be some mistake...I did not make these transactions," she said, as she read over them.

"These records indicate that you've deposited almost half a million dollars into Abad Nasir's account less than two months ago," said Sam.

"I'm telling you, there has to be a mistake. I did not make those transactions!" she shouted, with frustration.

"So, tell me...If you didn't make those transactions, then who did?" asked Sam. Rana didn't know what to say.

"I don't know, but it definitely was not me!" she said, getting upset.

"Ms. Denali, if you don't start cooperating with us, things will go very badly for you," said Sam. Ethan nodded his head at Sam. He got up and walked over to him.

"This isn't going anywhere. I think we need to bring these people in," said Ethan.

"You think that's a good idea?"

"Well, she's clearly hiding something...We might be able to get some answers if we stick her in a holding cell," said Ethan. Sam stood there and thought for a moment. He then looked at his wrist watch.

"You're right, we don't have a lot of time left. Let's do it," he said. He turned around and walked towards Rana.

"What's happening? Am I free to go?" she asked.

"Not exactly...Ms. Denali, I'm afraid I'm going to have to place you under arrest," he said. "I'm detaining you under the Anti-Terrorism Act of 2013." He went to take hold of her.

"But I haven't done anything wrong, please. This is a mistake!" she shouted, getting more upset. But Sam didn't want to hear it. He cuffed Rana and escorted her to the door. Ethan opened it and they came out with Rana in cuffs.

"What's happening?" asked Wendy.

"We're taking Ms. Denali back to our office for further questioning," said Sam.

"What the hell is going on?" said the angry voice of Daniel Carmichael. He came walking down the steps dressed in his black wedding attire and was shocked to see that his fiancé was in cuffs. Eric closed his eyes as he saw him.

"Sweetheart, calm down. It's nothing to worry about," said Wendy.

"Nothing to worry about? Why is my fiancé in hand cuffs?" he demanded. Ethan stepped in to take care of the situation.

"Sir, please calm down. We're detectives with the AFP. We're taking Ms. Denali to be questioned about her connections to a terrorist," he said.

"Oh, for fuck sake!" he shouted. "That's fucking bullshit, my fiancé doesn't know any terrorist!" he said, getting red in the face.

"Danny, please. You're not making this any easier," said Rana, as Sam continued walking to the exit.

"Will someone please explain what the fuck is going on?" he demanded. They all fell silent at that. Then, Eric came forward.

"I'll explain everything, just let them go, Danny," he said. Daniel didn't say anything at that. Ethan and Sam continued to walk towards the door. As he went to open the door, Wendy Carmichael caught up with them.

"Ma'am, I'm afraid you can't come with us," said Sam.

"You get your hands off me right now," she said, abruptly.

"I'm not only Rana's mother in law, but I'm also her lawyer…So, you can either let me come with you, or I will see you in court." Sam looked over at Ethan, and he slowly nodded. Then, the four of them headed out the door. Eric stood there looking shocked as the door closed.

Joe Parsons checked himself into a hotel in Sydney. He was annoyed at the fact that he couldn't stop Jeremy Stewart from going live with the story that would certainly destroy the President, along with his own career. As he settled in, he got out his laptop and turned it on. Joe started typing at his laptop. He was also expecting to meet with someone in a few moments who would hopefully help with his problem. As he sat there checking his emails, and glancing at the TV, there was a knock at the door. Joe looked up, and quickly muted the television. He went over to the door and peered through the look hole to see who it was. When he saw who was on the other side, he immediately opened it. "Harry, good to see you again," said Joe, shaking his hand. It was Harry Swanson who was an old friend of Joe's and he knew him quite well. They shook hands and Joe showed him in. "Can I get you something to drink, Harry?"

"No, I'm fine thanks Joe. Nice apartment."

"Thanks, just staying here while I'm in Sydney. On official business for the President," he said.

"How is she, anyway?"

"She's been better. A lot more stressed with this situation hanging over her," he said, and Harry nodded.

"So, just on that subject, what is it you want me to do, exactly? I wasn't quite sure what you needed me to do," he said. Joe paused for a moment.

"I can't go into specific details, Harry. But, suffice it to say, I need you to make someone disappear." Harry's eyes widened.

"You can't be serious, Joe? Who do you think I am? I'm not going to murder someone!" he snapped.

"Don't be ridiculous, Harry…That's not what I meant," said Joe.

"I just need you to take this person out of the public eye, keep him isolated for a few hours, and then let him go," said Joe. Harry thought about it for a moment.

"And this operation, it's been approved by the President?" he asked.

"Oh, yes, of course. She's completely behind it. As agreed, I've got your deposit fee of 25k." Joe reached over and grabbed a brown leather brief case. He turned it around and unlocked it, revealing several rows of notes.

"Once the job is done, I'll transfer the remainder to your account." Harry's eyes widened at the sight of the money.

"I'll take the job...What's the target?" he asked, as he gently moved his hands over the green notes. Joe grabbed the newspaper that was sitting on the side table; he placed it on top of the money. The front page had an image of Jeremy Stewart.

"Fuck me!" he cursed.

"You want that drink now, Harry?" asked Joe. Harry didn't say anything, he was in complete shock.

Eric Carmichael was still trying to get over what had just happened. Rana Denali had just been arrested by the Australian Federal Police, and now he was left to deal with one sticky situation. He was about to explain to his brother, Daniel Carmichael, about what was going on. He wasn't looking forward to it, but he knew that he'd eventually have to tell him. "So…You were going to tell me what the fuck is going on?" he said. Eric closed his eyes, and then turned around.

"Look, you're my brother, and I love you…But ever since you got together with Rana, I've been a bit concerned about her," he began. "I began to suspect that Rana was with you because she wanted the money, and it wasn't until she started work for the company, I noticed she'd been spending quite a bit of money," he said.

"Are you fucking serious?" said Daniel.

"Have you been spying on Rana?"

"I had to…I hired a private investigator because I was worried that Rana might be a…Terrorist," he said. Daniel's eyes closed.

"My fucking God…Have you completely lost your mind?" said Daniel.

"You need to understand that I did this because I care about you…You're my brother, Danny," he said.

"You hired a fucking private investigator? Why in God's name would you do that?" he demanded.

"Because, Danny…The investigator found out that she'd been supporting a terrorist using the company's finances," he explained. Daniel just shook his head in disbelief.

"I don't believe this, Eric…Just because I'm getting married and you're not, doesn't give you the right to ruin my wedding day!" they both fell silent after that.

"Danny, I'm sorry…But I don't trust Rana. She's been lying to us!" he said.

"I don't care if you're sorry, Eric…You spied on Rana! I will never forgive you for this!" he shouted. Daniel just stormed off in a huff.

After the arrest, Detectives Sam Hunter and Ethan Cooper returned to the Serious Crimes Unit. Rana Denali was not happy. She had been put in one of the agency's interview rooms. Wendy Carmichael was there with her too and attempting to calm her down. She was getting rather agitated by the whole situation and couldn't believe that she was being suspected of being involved with terrorism. Chief Inspector Mick Greer opened the door and went into the viewing room. It was a small room attached to the interview room with a double-sided window. "So, what's happening?" asked Mick, as the door closed. Ethan and Sam were in the room and were monitoring Rana.

"We've been sweating her for the past ten minutes. She's getting frustrated by the idea of being connected to a terrorist," said Sam.

"Has she said anything yet?"

"No. Just coming up with a lot of excuses, and commotion," said Ethan. Mick checked his watch. "So, how's Simon settling in?" he asked, changing the subject.

"He seems to be coping okay. Somewhat quiet," said Mick.

"That's Simon…He's probably just nervous," Ethan replied. They didn't say anything after that.

"Alright, we're going to have to get this over with, we don't have a whole lot of time," said Mick. Then he went over and opened the door to the interview room.

As he went in, Rana stood up.

"I demand to know what is going on!" Rana shouted.

"Ms. Denali, I'm Chief Inspector Mick Greer, the head of this department."

"Good, finally someone with authority," said Wendy. "This is absolutely ridiculous. Your officers had no right coming into our house and arresting an innocent woman," she added.

"Mrs. Carmichael, please do not interrupt!" Mick shouted. "Ms. Denali is being questioned because of her connection to a terrorist, Abad Nasir...We have evidence that suggests Ms. Denali has been financially supporting Abad Nasir," said Mick. He then also showed her bank statements with large sums of money being withdrawn. "We managed to trace the funds to Abad Nasir's personal bank account...How do you explain that?" he demanded. Rana didn't know what to say. Her eyes were slowly filling with tears.

"I can't tell you anymore than I already know...I did not make those transactions, and I don't know this Abad Nasir!" she shouted, getting more upset.

"The evidence is telling us otherwise...Ms. Denali, we have intelligence that confirms a terrorist group is planning to detonate a radiological dirty bomb in the middle of Sydney!" he shouted. Rana's eyes widened. "Tens of thousands of innocent lives are at stake, here! Now we need you to start cooperating, or you're going to spend the rest of your life in prison!" he bellowed. Rana was completely shaken by all of this. "Now, I'm going to give you half an hour to revise your story, and then I want to know the truth!" he said. He then got up and went over to the door. After stepping through, he slammed it shut behind him.

"Not exactly what I thought was going to happen," said Sam.

"We have to give her something to think about...With the thought of thousands of lives at stake, it might entice her to come clean," said Mick. "In the meantime, I'm going to update the Commissioner," he added, and then headed out the other door.

Marc Cameron had never been more scared in his entire life. He was being watched by several men armed with guns and found to be quite intimidating. Especially since he was being forced to build a nuclear weapon. Marc spent the last half an hour soldering electrical wires that were connected to the device's detonator. Of course, he wasn't working alone; Matthias Granger also had an expert of his own and he was assisting Marc with the nuclear material. There were twenty or so uranium fuel rods and each were placed up against a large cylindrical object. The entire time he was working, he couldn't stop thinking about his family, and worried if they were okay. Across the other side of the warehouse, Matthias sat at his desk. He was keeping a close eye on Marc Cameron and kept checking his watch. As he sat there, his blackberry phone started ringing. It was a private number, so he answered it. "Yes?"

"It's me," a masculine voice answered. Matthias knew exactly who it was.

"Why are you calling? You know it's risky to call."

"I know. But I had no choice…I'm in a bit of trouble."

"What kind of trouble?"

"It's my brother…He's hired a private investigator. He suspects Rana of being a terrorist. The AFP just arrested her." Matthias' eyes widened.

"How did your brother find out?"

"I've got no idea. But Eric seemed to have adopted Dad's inquisitive nature," said Daniel Carmichael. There was a pause on the other end.

"Do they suspect you're involved?"

"No, not at this point, but if they keep digging, they might find out."

"Alright. By the time they do, it'll be too late," said Matthias. "The weapon is almost ready. It will be delivered to you soon. Keep alert," he said.

"I will…Thank you Matthias." Then the call disconnected. He put away his phone and then got up to check on Marc Cameron.

"Mr. Cameron, how much longer before the device is completed?" he asked, as he approached Marc. He looked up and removed his glasses.

"It…Should be done in half an hour," he replied. "You'd better make that fifteen minutes," said Matthias, with a sinister grin. Marc's lip began to tremble.

Watching from afar, Diane Faulkner could see Matthias standing there talking to Marc. She was becoming concerned after she found out that Matthias was planning to attack the Harbour Bridge. She had to figure out a way to contact the SCU, but it wasn't exactly going to be easy. There were men all over the place taking guard with their machine guns. She thought for a moment and then looked over to see Stuart Mason standing out the front having a cigarette. She walked over to join.

"Hey, mind if I join you?" she asked. Stuart chuckled and then handed her one. She lit it up and took a couple of drags.

"You're full of surprises, Kelly. Didn't know you smoked," said Stuart.

"Only when I'm stressed," she replied.

"Why are you stressed?" Diane took another drag of her cigarette.

"Just can't believe that I've finally met Matthias," she said. "I wasn't sure what to expect."

"Now that you've met him, what did you expect?"

"Not someone good looking," she replied, and Stuart chuckled. "Can I ask you a question?"

"Sure."

"Do you agree with what we're doing here?" she asked. Mason looked at her oddly.

"What do you mean?"

"I mean, do you agree with what Matthias is doing, and wants to do? All those people we're going to kill," she said.

"We're fighting a cause," he said. "People have to die for the greater good, even if they are innocent." Diane didn't know what to say about that. Then Mason put out his cigarette. "Come on, we need to get ready for the next stage in the operation." He started walking back into the warehouse. Diane was starting to freak out as she tried to find ways of contacting the SCU. She too put out her cigarette and followed Stuart. Once they got back inside, Matthias was standing there waiting.

"Good of you to join us, Miss Duncan," said Matthias. "I want you to go with Mr. Mason and deliver a package to one of my operatives. He lives in Mosman. I'll text you the address once you've left," he said.

"Kelly, let's go," Stuart called out. She slowly walked over to the van and climbed into the passenger seat. Stuart climbed into the driver's seat and turned on the ignition. After buckling up, he slowly drove out of the main entrance of warehouse. Matthias stood there watching with a big grin on his face. He was pleased that his operation was on schedule.

Eric Carmichael was still upset by what had happened. He was starting to get anxious and began pacing the kitchen floor. Daniel had disappeared for the last twenty or so minutes and was probably sulking in his room like a five-year-old. He hadn't heard anything from his mother, so something must be happening. He thought for a moment and then went over to the computer. After logging in, he wanted to find out what exactly his private investigator found. He signed in to the company's corporate bank account and began searching through recent transactions made. There were several bank transactions that added up to a total of five hundred thousand dollars. He thought for a moment and then took out his mobile phone to dial a number. "Aaron Morgan," he answered.

"Aaron, it's Eric Carmichael. The AFP just arrested Rana Denali...Are you sure the information you got was correct?" he asked.

"Yes, we double checked it with ASIO and they confirmed it with the Department of Immigration...Rana Denali did in fact transfer that money to Abad Nasir's account."

"I'm still not convinced that she did."

"Look, I realize you're having doubts about this. But the fact is, ASIO confirmed the information was accurate. There's no other explanation," said Aaron.

"What if she's being set up?" he thought.

"I don't follow?"

"I mean, what if someone wanted us to find out that she'd been helping the terrorists?"

"I don't see how that's possible. It would take a considerably smart person to come up with something like that," said Aaron. Eric let out a sigh of frustration.

"I just feel bad for my brother that's all...I'm starting to regret this whole thing," he said.

"I understand…But if the AFP are questioning Rana Denali, then you should feel good about potentially stopping a terrorist attack," said Aaron.

"I know, I should…Look, I should go. I still need to figure out what I'm going to say to Daniel," he said.

"Thanks for your help Aaron."

"No problem. Call me if you need any more help," said Aaron, and then hung up. After he put down the phone, he sat there and thought for a moment. He then looked up to see Daniel standing there. He didn't look too pleased with Eric.

"Danny, I'm glad you're here. I just wanted to say that I'm sorry for what's happening. I didn't mean for this to ruin your wedding day," he said.

"You just couldn't help yourself, could you?" he said. "You couldn't leave well enough alone." Eric didn't say anything.

"I just wish you didn't go snooping around, because I didn't expect you to find anything." At that, Daniel pulled a handgun on Eric. He cocked the gun and aimed it at Eric's head. Eric's eyes widened with shock, and his face went as white as a ghost.

"Danny, what the hell are you doing?" he said.

"Put your hands up, Eric," he demanded. Eric was reluctant at first. "I said, put your fucking hands up!" he shouted, as he walked up to him. Eric jumped and quickly raised his hands.

"Danny, I don't understand. What's going on?" he asked.

"You see, that's what really amuses me about you…You never have any idea about what's going on," said. Then, Eric started to realize what was happening.

"It, was you? You're working for the terrorists?" he said. Daniel didn't reply straight away, and grinned.

"Why?"

"Because people like Abad Nasir know what's really going on. He opened my eyes, Eric. He showed me what this government is really like…They're criminals," he said.

"I don't believe what I'm hearing," said Eric. "You sound like an insane fanatic."

"No, I'm a true believer in the cause of freedom and just," he said. Eric was starting to get upset.

"So, what are you going to do to me? Kill me?" said Eric. Daniel just stared at his brother, still holding the gun at his head, and held his finger on the trigger.

Rana Denali was still in shock at the fact that a terrorist group were planning to detonate a dirty bomb in Sydney. She couldn't get over that tens of thousands of innocent people would suffer. But she was still annoyed at the AFP as they still believed she was working for the terrorists. No matter what she said, they were not convinced. Rana was still being held in the interview room at the Serious Crimes Unit. Wendy Carmichael was with her and continued to try and calm her down. On the main floor, everyone was still busy trying to track down the terrorists and stop them from setting off the dirty bomb. Chief Inspector Mick Greer walked across the floor and went into the agency's briefing room. Detective Sergeant Simon Harper and Felicity Meyers were inside and doing some analysis on Rana Denali's background. Felicity Meyers was there helping them also. "So, have you found anything yet?" asked Mick, as he came into the room.

"Nothing out of the ordinary. We know she's an immigrant from the Middle-East. Her family moved here when she was ten years old. She graduated from the University of Sydney with a Bachelor of Economics. She then secured a position with Carmichael Prospecting as the Chief Financial Officer in 2011," said Felicity. "She's been with the company ever since."

"There's nothing in her profile that suggests she's been involved with terrorists. Yes, she's from the Middle-East, and yes, she's Muslim, but that doesn't confirm she's a terrorist," said Simon.

"There must be a connection somewhere. ASIO confirmed she transferred more than five hundred thousand dollars to Abad Nasir's bank account," said Mick.

"We've been looking into that, and it seems there's some inconsistencies with those transactions," said Simon. Mick looked at her, oddly.

"What kind of inconsistencies?"

"Well, after analysing the transactions, we discovered that the most recent transaction made totalled up to ninety thousand dollars. However, this transaction was made two months ago at a local branch in Sydney," Felicity commented.

"What's unusual about that?"

"According to the bank's records, the person who made those transactions was not Rana Denali…She was in fact out of the country on the day the transaction was made," said Felicity. He showed Mick the paperwork to prove it.

"So, if Rana Denali didn't authorize these transactions, then who did?" asked Mick. They all looked at each other, with blank expressions.

Eric Carmichael couldn't believe that his brother, Daniel Carmichael was a terrorist. All this time, he suspected Rana Denali of being a terrorist because she was a Muslim from the Middle-East. Eric had been tied up to a chair and taken into the garage. Daniel finished tying his wrists and then placed duct tape over his mouth. As he did so, his mobile phone started ringing. "Hello?" he answered.

"Daniel, it's Matthias. What's your status?"

"I'm almost ready. I had to deal with a situation, but it's all good now." There was a pause.

"What situation?" Eric let out a sigh.

"It's my brother…He found out about my involvement. I had to neutralize him," said Daniel.

"That's unfortunate. But it's not a concern right now…Mr. Mason is on his way over with the package. He should be arriving momentarily. You need to be ready to leave ASAP," said Matthias. Daniel didn't reply straight away. He looked over his shoulder as he heard a vehicle pulling up outside.

"I think they just arrived. I should go."

"Okay, good. And remember, you're doing this for the cause." Daniel smiled.

"I know." Then he hung up. He thought for a moment and looked over at Eric who was still sitting there in the chair, tied up. He shook his head and then went over to the garage door. At the press of a button, the door rolled up, and sunlight beamed in. Parked on the side of the road was a black vehicle. Daniel walked over to it and Stuart Mason climbed out.

"You must be Daniel Carmichael?" asked Mason, and he slowly nodded. Diane was sitting in the front passenger seat. She could see Daniel talking with Stuart and had a perfect shot of his face. She quickly got out her Smartphone and snapped a photo of Daniel Carmichael. She watched as Stuart handed Daniel the case.

"Matthias wants you at the target ASAP," said Stuart.

"I know. I'm ready to leave now. Is the explosive in the truck?" said Daniel.

"Yes. The timer has been set. As soon as you get to the target, use this remote to activate the device," said Stuart, as he handed Daniel a small remote. Diane was watching them the whole time. Stuart and Daniel stared at each other for a few moments.

Then, Mason handed him the keys. Stuart went over to Diane's side. She opened the door.

"What's happening?" she asked.

"Daniel is heading to the target. We've got other things to do," he said, and then started up the car. At the same time,

Diane looked through the side mirror and she saw the Transit van driving off.

After they'd delivered the package to Daniel Carmichael, Stuart Mason and Diane Faulkner made their way back into the city. They took a taxi into the city and went to the nearest hotel. It was a nice hotel room with a beautiful view of the harbour and a luxurious Queen-sized bed with an en-suite. They'd only booked the room for an hour or so, because they had just had sex. Ever since Diane Faulkner worked undercover with the UAG cell twelve weeks ago, Diane had a sexual fling with Stuart Mason. She didn't want to get involved with something, particularly since he was a criminal, but it was her only way into the group. Diane and Stuart were lying in bed, naked, with just the sheet covering their bodies. Stuart sat up and grabbed a cigarette from his packet and lit it up. He seemed to be a bit worried about Diane, as she didn't seem like herself lately. "Are you alright, Kelly?" he asked, as he took a couple of drags. Diane lay there curled up with the sheet tucked under her arms.

"I'm fine, why wouldn't I be?" she replied.

"You tell me...You just seem a bit distant lately," he said. Diane didn't reply straight away. She then rolled over and sat up to take a cigarette.

"No, I'm fine. Honestly," she said.

"We just got the biggest pay check ever. I'd expect you to be a bit more enthusiastic," said Stuart. She paused for a moment. She got out of bed and started getting dressed again.

"I did at first…But then I realized I wasn't going to be able to spend it," she said. Stuart looked confused.

"Why's that?"

"Because you're about to be arrested." She closed her eyes, and her heart dropped. Stuart had no idea what she was on about. Just then, the hotel room door flew open. About six AFP counter-terrorist officers stormed the room with their guns raised and pointed them at Stuart Mason.

"Armed Police! Armed Police!" they shouted. "Stuart Mason, you are under arrest...Put your hands on your head!" Stuart had no choice but to do so. The officers immediately arrested him and detained him. SCU Detectives Sam Hunter and Ethan Cooper entered the room and approached Diane Faulkner, who stood by the window feeling kind of overwhelmed by all of this.

"Hey Dee, are you okay?" asked Sam. Diane turned around.

"Yeah, I'm fine. Just still in a bit of shock that's all," she said. She looked over at Stuart who was being led out of the room by the officers.

"Did you find out where Matthias is?" said Ethan.

"Yes, but there's something else. Matthias is planning another terrorist attack. It's going down soon," she said, "I managed to take a photo of the bomber." She grabbed her phone and opened the photograph of Daniel Carmichael. She showed it to Ethan and Sam, and their faces went white as a sheet.

"Jesus. Are you sure that's right?" said Sam.

"Yeah, of course. I saw him less than fifteen minutes ago, why?"

"We know who he is…His name's Daniel Carmichael. He's the fiancé of Rana Denali," said Sam. "We detained her this morning because we received intelligence from ASIO that she was supporting a terrorist called Abad Nasir," said Ethan. Diane's eyes widened.

"Fuck…Well clearly, she wasn't the terrorist."

"What's the target?" asked Ethan, as he got out his phone to start dialling a number.

"It's the Harbour Bridge. He left for the target about ten minutes ago, so he could be already there," she said. Ethan was calling Mick Greer.

"This is Detective Chief Inspector Mick Greer."

"Hey, it's Ethan. We just got to Diane. She's fine. But we just found out that Matthias is planning another attack," he said.

"Bloody hell. Do we know how it's happening, what the target is?"

"Yeah. She said the target is the Harbour Bridge," said Ethan. "Boss, there's one more thing…The bomber is Daniel Carmichael." There was a sudden pause.

"Are you serious?"

"I know, I couldn't believe it either. But Dee has a photo of Daniel meeting with Stuart Mason. They delivered him a bomb," he said.

"Son of a bitch...Okay, I'll have an armed response team dispatched to the bridge," said Mick. handgun, and loaded it.

Meanwhile, Daniel Carmichael was being the wheel of the Transit van. He was heading towards the city and had just passed Milsons Point Station. In the back of the van was a massive explosive device. Traffic was building up now as he got closer to the bridge. The whole time he was driving, he thought about what he was doing, and what he'd done to his brother. But he was true to the cause and did not want to let Matthias down. He was chosen specifically for this task, and he was prepared to go down in the history books. The traffic was starting to get denser as he got closer to the bridge. He'd just got onto the onramp and was approaching the first set of traffic lights. He was starting to sweat as he checked his watch and saw that it was approaching midday. The bomb was set to go off at exactly twelve o'clock.

At the SCU Operations Centre, Chief Inspector Mick Greer came walking out of his office. He was walking rather swiftly with a sense of urgency in his step. He was heading over to Felicity's station, and at the same time, he was talking on the phone with the Premier of New South Wales. "With respect, Premier. I believe it's the right decision to shut down the bridge," he said. "Because Sir, I have reason to believe that the bridge is the target for a terrorist attack. It came directly from one of my detectives in the field. We recently apprehended a terrorist suspect," said Mick. "We need to act now, Sir. Dozens of lives are at stake. You need to shut the bridge down now...Thank you," he finished, and hung up the phone.

"What was that about?" asked Felicity.

"Daniel Carmichael is the terrorist. He's planning to blow up the Harbour Bridge. I was just trying to convince the Premier to shut it down before it's too late," he said. "Have you got any drones in the area?"

"Yes, there's one just off Kurraba Point. I'll redirect it now," she said. She was at the controls of one of the SCU's aerial surveillance drones. She turned the controls to the left and she could see the Harbour Bridge in the distance.

"What exactly are we looking for?"

"The bomb will probably be in a medium to large size vehicle. We need to find it now," he said. Felicity lowered the drone to two thousand feet and she zoomed the camera in on the bridge. She was looking at the screen and tried to identify a medium sized vehicle. There were a lot of trucks and big vehicles, which would prove difficult to find it.

"This is insane...It's going to be like looking for a needle in a haystack," said Felicity.

"I know, but it's our only chance at stopping an attack." Meanwhile, Daniel Carmichael was driving the van. He was approaching the middle of the bridge, and it was almost midday. Daniel's heart was racing. There were dozens of cars in front of him, and as he looked through his rear-view mirror, he could see dozens of cars behind him. The bomb's timer was ticking away and getting closer to zero.

He checked his watch one more time, and knew it was the right moment. He suddenly hit the brakes and swung the wheel to the left. The van swerved and stopped on an angle right in the centre of the bridge. Cars behind him swerved to dodge the van, while some stopped out of confusion as to what was going. Within a split second, Daniel pressed the button on the trigger, and the device exploded.

It was the most horrifying event to take place. News of the catastrophic terrorist attack on the Sydney Harbour Bridge, soon travelled across the entire country. News channels across the nation were covering the attack and stating that it was the worst attack on Australian soil since the 2020 Independence Day attack. The reports were stating that upwards of one hundred and fifty people were killed in the explosion. When the bomb went off, the explosion crippled the bridge's integrity and caused it to collapse. At the Serious Crimes Unit, everyone was in complete shock by what had happened. They were all standing there gaping at the screens that were displaying news reports on the attack. Simon was standing by his desk and watched the news. It was the most horrifying event to take place. News of the catastrophic terrorist attack on the Sydney Harbour Bridge, soon travelled across the entire country. The reports were stating that upwards of one hundred and fifty people were killed in the explosion. When the bomb went off, the explosion crippled the bridge's integrity and caused it to collapse. At the Serious Crimes Unit, everyone was in complete shock by what had happened. They were all standing there gaping at the screens that were displaying news reports on the attack. Simon was standing by his desk and watched the news.

News of the terrorist attack made its way over to Canberra, more specifically, the Government House, and the President of Australia had been alerted. The President of Australia, Christine Mills, was in her office. She was in utter shock as she watched the TV in awe; she could see a live news report of the Sydney Harbour Bridge, and a plume of smoke rising from the centre of the bridge. The report was showing an aerial view of the bridge, with alarming headlines. The headlines read: 'Terrorist bomb at Harbour Bridge. Hundreds feared dead', and a reporter was giving updates about the situation; she just couldn't believe this had happened. As she stood there watching the news report with tears filling her eyes, there was a knock at the door. Joe Parsons entered and saw her staring at the TV. He too was shocked by all of this. "Your Excellency, I came back as soon as I heard," he said. Joe had just returned from Sydney. "Are you okay?" he asked.

She didn't say anything at first, and then slowly turned around looking upset. She went over and sat down at her desk. "Ma'am?" he said, again. She finally looked up.

"Not really, Joe. I can't believe this is happening," she said, and Joe slowly nodded. "Has there been any word on how many

"I've spoken with the AFP Commissioner...He's saying that it was a terrorist attack, most likely a UAG cell," he explained. Christine didn't say anything. She was in too much shock by all of this.

"How did it go in Sydney?" she asked. Joe didn't reply straight away. He was caught off guard.

"Ah, it was fine, but we don't need to talk about that now. It can wait," he said. Christine looked back at the TV. She was in utter disbelief that something like this happened.

At the Serious Crimes Unit, everyone was rushing about trying to get on top of their tasks. There was certainly a lot of activity since the attack on the Harbour Bridge shook the entire city. All the agency's TV screens were showing news reports of the destroyed Harbour Bridge. Detectives Ethan Cooper and Sam Hunter returned to the agency. Diane Faulkner was with them and she was glad to be back at the office. But the three were also in shock by what had happened. Diane was still getting over the fact that her undercover operation was over and readjusting herself with the real world. Stuart Mason had been taken down to one of the agency's interview rooms where he was put under guard and awaiting to be questioned. The three of them walked across the floor and made their way over to Mick Greer's office. He was currently talking on the phone with the AFP Assistant Commissioner. "Alright, I'll keep you updated." He hung up and looked at the three exhausted detectives. "Diane, excellent work with the undercover operation," he said, and she nodded. Detective Simon Harper came over to the group. "And this is?" asked Simon.

"Oh, yes. Diane, this Detective Sergeant Simon Harper. He's recently joined the task force," said Mick. Simon reached over and shook hands with Diane.

"Pleasure to meet you, Detective Faulkner," said Simon.

"Likewise," Diane replied. There was an awkward silence after that. Ethan looked over at Simon.

"Did you manage to find out where Matthias Granger is hiding out?" asked Mick.

"Yes, I did. Matthias' base of operations is at the Carriage works tram sheds. It's an abandoned warehouse, but I don't know exactly where it is."

"Okay good. I'll have Felicity re-task a drone over the site," said Mick.

"I've just been talking with the Commissioner...It seems that more than a hundred and fifty people were reportedly killed in the attack," he said. All three detectives' mouths dropped.

"I can't believe this is happening," said Diane. She felt partially responsible because she knew about the attack and she couldn't do anything to stop it.

"I know this is a lot to take in, but we need to stay focused," said Mick. They paused for a moment.

"What's happening with Rana Denali?" asked Sam. Mick didn't reply straight away.

"After finding out that it was in fact Daniel Carmichael who was the terrorist, I have no choice but to release her," he said. The room fell silent after that. He got up and started walking to the door.

"In the meantime, I need you all to submit your briefing report." The three of them followed him out and made their way back to their desks. Mick on the other hand went down the corridor to the interview room where Rana Denali was still waiting. He opened the door and went in. She immediately stood up, still angry.

"I demand to know what's going on!" she said, getting upset.

"Ms. Denali, please sit down…I'm afraid I have some bad news," said Mick. Rana slowly sat down. "Mrs. Carmichael, this concerns you as well. It's to do with your son, Daniel."

"What about my son, what's happened to him?"

"There's been a major terrorist attack here in Sydney…A bomb just went off at the Harbour Bridge," he said. "We believe more than a hundred people were killed in the bombing." The room fell silent after that. Rana didn't know how to respond.

"My God," Rana gasped.

"What does this have to do with my son?" asked Wendy. Mick didn't reply straight away.

"There's no easy way for me to say this. Your son was the shooter." Wendy's heart sank. Her eyes started filling with tears.

"What are you saying?"

"Your son was the one who set off the bomb," said Mick. Wendy shook her head in disbelief. Tears filling her eye lids.

"I don't understand...My son can't be a terrorist," she said, getting upset.

"I'm afraid it's true...In light of this, Ms. Denali, all criminal charges against you have been dropped, and you are no longer under investigation...You're free to go," he said. Rana didn't say anything. She was too upset by all of this.

Matthias Granger was pleased at the fact that his operation was going according to plan. He stood by one of the metal support beams next to his workstation. The TV was on and it showed an aerial shot of the convention centre. He was pleased to find out that the terrorist attack on the Sydney Harbour Bridge was a complete success. It was something that he'd been trying to achieve ever since the downfall of his previous financial benefactor, Birchall McClelland; it was the cell's main goal to carry out politically motivated violence and cause chaos, and now, Matthias Granger had achieved that goal. Matthias made his way over to where Marc Cameron was working on the dirty bomb and he seemed to be nearing completion. "Dr. Cameron, how much longer until the device is ready?" he asked. Marc stopped working and removed his glasses as he looked up.

"About five more minutes," he replied, and Matthias grinned. His face was bloodied and bruised since he was beaten up by Matthias' men.

"Good. Then you should continue." He turned and walked over to one of his men. Adam Cochran was one of Matthias' trusted lieutenants, and he was the one who was going to be delivering the dirty bomb to its target. He was standing next to a blue Transit van with its back doors open. Matthias approached him. "Are you ready to leave?" he asked, and Adam slowly nodded.

"Yes. I'm ready to carry out this mission," said Adam.

"Good…Once you get to the location, this phone will ring twice. That will be a signal for you to arm the bomb," he said. He handed Adam a mobile. "If there's no answer after four rings, then you know it's time to activate the timer," he added. Adam placed the phone in his pocket.

"Matthias!" a voice called out from behind. Matthias turned around to see another one of his men come over. "The bomb is ready." Matthias smiled. Then, several more men came over and were carrying the dirty bomb which was on a trolley as it was quite heavy. Matthias stood there and watched on as the bomb was loaded into the back of the van. Once it was securely loaded, the doors were closed, and Adam shook hands with Matthias. Adam climbed into the driver's side and turned on the ignition. At that, the van slowly drove off.

After talking with Rana Denali, Mick Greer came out of the interview room. He made his way back over to Felicity's workstation. She'd been busy on her computer and finally managed to re-task one of the agency's aerial surveillance drones. The drone was hovering about five thousand feet in the air and moved over the carriage works complex. As well as being a surveillance drone, it was equipped with specialist infra-red technology which enabled Felicity to scan a building and see how many people were inside it. Mick came over to her and leaned over her shoulder. "So, what've we got?" he asked, as he looked at her screen.

"I re-tasked one of the drones. Infra-red scan shows there's approximately twenty heat-signatures in one of the warehouses," said Felicity. "The drone also picked up small traces of radioactive material."

"Which means that's where Matthias is, as well as the material," said Mick, and Felicity nodded.

"Looks that way." Mick thought for a moment.

"Okay, I'm going to send in a tactical unit." Mick took out his phone and started dialling a number. "This is Chief Inspector Mick Greer. I'm authorizing a counter-terrorist strike team. Coordinates will be forwarded momentarily," he said, and hung up. "Get those coordinates to the tactical unit." Felicity nodded. Meanwhile, Simon Harper was watching as Mick spoke with Felicity. He thought for a moment and then looked around. He could see personnel walking around getting on with their jobs, even though there was a crisis ensuing. He thought for a moment, and then got up to head off. He made his way down the corridor and went into the IT server room. He locked the door and took out his mobile to dial a number. It rang a few times, and then a voice answered.

"Yes?" a deep voice answered. Simon paused before responding.

"Matthias, it's me…There's a problem," he said.

"What problem is that, Detective Harper?" said the voice of Matthias Granger.

"SCU found your location…They're sending a tactical unit to arrest you as we speak," he said.

"How is that possible?"

"The SCU had an operative working for you undercover. Diane Faulkner. She infiltrated your cell twelve weeks ago. She only just came back in," he said. There was another pause on the line.

"Are you saying she's law enforcement?"

"Yes. She was planted there twelve weeks ago," he said.

"I would've told you sooner, but it would have tipped off the agency there was a traitor," said Simon.

"That's still unacceptable, Detective Harper," said Matthias. "You should have warned me sooner."

"I know, I'm sorry. But the point is, you need to leave as soon as possible. The teams will be at your location in less than ten minutes," said Simon.

"Damn it. If I'm captured, the operation will fail...I'll make arrangements to leave. The dirty bomb will be in position shortly," said Matthias.

"Good. I'll keep you updated." Then Detective Sergeant Simon Harper disconnected the call.

Adam Cochran drove the blue Transit van into the city centre. It only took him about five minutes to get there and he arrived at the specific location. Adam parked the van which contained the radiological dirty bomb in the back of the van. He parked the van in a narrow alley near Sydney's Martin Place Railway Station. Since there was a terrorist attack less than a kilometre away, there were not many people in the city. He parked the van about five hundred metres away from the station's entrance. He sat there for a few moments and climbed into the back to sit next to the dirty bomb. There wasn't much room in the back as it was quite large and took up most of it. About five minutes went by. Just then, Adam's phone started ringing. It made him jump, but he knew who it was; it rang twice which made him armed the bomb. He set the timer for fifteen minutes. The bomb had a visual digital timer on the front of it. His phone kept ringing and made four rings. The ringing finally stopped, and Adam activated the timer. It began ticking down from fifteen minutes. 14:59:59…14:59:58…14:59:57.

Detectives Ethan Cooper and Sam Hunter arrived at the Carriage-works warehouse complex. They pulled up in an SCU vehicle and a black van pulled up behind them. As it stopped, twelve counter-terrorist officers climbed out. They were dressed in full combat gear and held tactical shields. Ethan and Sam were gearing up with Kevlar vests and loading their Glock 19 handguns. The Tactical Response officers were getting themselves ready for an assault on the warehouse where Matthias Granger was hiding out. Five minutes had passed, and they knew they were running out of time before the bomb detonated. The tactical response officers formed into a line and entered the warehouse complex. Ethan and Sam were trailing behind them; both wore protective vests and had their Glock 19 handguns ready. They approached the main entrance to the warehouse, and steadily entered. The warehouse was dark, but the officers were equipped with flash lights. There were stacks of containers and crates set up in a maze. The officers began to search the large warehouse. Unbeknownst to the officers, and his men were hiding in various places around the warehouse. They were armed to the teeth with G-36 assault rifles and were getting ready for an armed assault. Just then, the tactical officers stopped as a grenade bounced near them. Within a split second, the grenade exploded, killing several of the others. Moments after, Matthias' men unleashed gunfire on the officers. Ethan and Sam immediately took cover behind one of the crates. Even though they were struggling to see in the dark, they open-fired in the direction of the rapid gunfire.

Christine Mills was still shocked by what happened. She couldn't believe that terrorists carried out an attack on the Sydney Harbour Bridge, and that so many innocent people were killed. She was in her office at the Government House and the TV was still on. It continued to show news reports of the horrifying events that had transpired. She was finding it difficult to concentrate on her work. Right now, she was currently on the phone talking with the Prime Minister of Australia and dealing with emergency response teams. The President was consulting with the Prime Minister about instigating a state of emergency. As she spoke, her Official Secretary, Joe Parsons entered. "Yes, thank you, Prime Minister. I appreciate your support. Keep me informed," she said. "Goodbye." Joe stood in front of her desk, waiting. "Joe…I was just talking with the Prime Minister. He's making plans to instigate a national state of emergency," she said.

"I think that's a good idea. Right now, we're dealing with a terrorist incident. If there's another attack planned, a state of emergency would be beneficial," said Joe, and Christine nodded.

"Yes, the PM agrees. He's going to announce it during the press conference." Joe nodded. The room fell silent after that. "So, I asked you about Sydney," she said. Joe paused. "You didn't tell me what happened?" she asked.

"Yes, sorry, I got side tracked…Do you really think this is a good time, Ma'am?" he said. Christine's eyebrow raised.

"I sent you there to take care of a problem, now I want to know what happened," she said. Joe didn't reply straight away and let out a sigh.

"Let's just say, the problem has been taken care of. Jeremy Stewart won't be able to publish the story any time soon," he replied. Christine looked at him, confused.

"And what exactly does that mean, Joe?"

"It's better you don't know the truth, Ma'am. It might back fire."

"Joe, I'm the President of Australia, I demand to know what the hell is going on?" she snapped. Of course, Joe was reluctant to tell her.

"Alright, fine, I'll tell you…After I met with Jeremy, he refused to hold off on publishing the story, so I knew I had to go to the next level to keep this story from coming to the surface," he said, and Christine nodded.

"Go on."

"I contacted an old friend of mine…I paid him to silence Jeremy Stewart," he said. Then, Christine's eyes widened.

"Oh my, God, Joe! You did not pay someone to kill Jeremy Stewart?" she yelled.

"No, no, of course not!" Joe was getting frustrated. "I paid someone to keep him hidden for a few hours."

"In other words, you kidnapped him?" she said, and Joe slowly nodded. "I can't believe what I'm hearing, Joe…This is outrageous!"

"I did what I had to, Christine! If Jeremy Stewart had published that story, your career would be over!" he shouted, getting red in the face.

"And what do you think is going to happen when he finds out you had him kidnapped? Joe, you could go to prison!" she said.

"It's not going to get that far, Ma'am…The person I hired is an old friend of mine. I trust him to make sure he gets the job done," said Joe. Christine just stood there. She couldn't believe what he was saying and shook her head.

"I don't know if I can trust you anymore, Joe...I don't want to deal with this right now. I'll call you if I need you," she said. Joe didn't say anything. He turned and headed to the door, feeling sorry for himself.

Ethan and Sam were still being pinned down by the rapid gunfire. The assault had been going on for the past five minutes or so and Ethan was getting impatient. He knew that this had to end soon so they could locate the dirty bomb. It was getting to a point where the tactical response officers were getting overwhelmed. They were outnumbered by the hostiles, and several of the officers were gunned down. But as they feared the worst, the roof of the warehouse began to vibrate. Two Australian Army Sikorsky S-70 helicopters hovered overhead. Each of the choppers contained a dozen counter-terrorism commandos armed with assault rifles. The choppers hovered over the roof of the warehouse; ropes were draped over the sides and simultaneously, the commandos' abseiled down the ropes. One by one, they landed safely on the roof. Then, as group, they made their way inside. Using their night-vision goggles, the commandos were able to identify the hostiles within seconds. Several grenades were thrown in the direction of a group of hostiles and were severely injured by the blast. With the added force of twenty-four commandos, Matthias and his men were soon overrun, and subsequently surrendered. After engaging in hand-to-hand combat, Matthias reluctantly gave up and he was arrested.

Ethan Cooper was exhausted after the punch-up and was getting himself ready to interrogate Matthias. "Matthias Granger, you're under arrest for conspiracy to carry out an act of terrorism, and the murder of more than two hundred innocent people," said Detective Sergeant Sam Hunter. A Tactical Response officer placed Matthias on a metal chair. Matthias was bloodied and scarred from the fight. Ethan Cooper came over to him and looked down at him with an angry expression on his face.

"Ethan, are you going to be okay with questioning him?" asked Sam. Ethan didn't reply straight away.

"Yeah, I'm fine," he said. "You're a son of a bitch, Matthias," he said. Of course, Matthias didn't say anything. "Tell me where the bomb is," he demanded. Matthias just responded with a spit of blood which landed near Ethan's foot. "Tell me where the bomb is!"

"Why should I tell you?" Matthias spoke, softly. Ethan struck him across the face, again. "No matter what you do to me, Cooper. I'll never help you…I'm doing this because this country is pathetic!" Matthias yelled. Ethan paused and then looked over at Sam. He grinned and turned back to Matthias.

"Oh, I think you'll reconsider," he said. Ethan started walking away and dialled a number.

"Chief Inspector Mick Greer."

"Hey Boss, it's Ethan. We've apprehended Matthias Granger. We also captured six of his men."

"That's good work Ethan. Has he told you where the dirty bomb is?" asked Mick. He was a little thrown off by what Ethan said.

"No. He's refusing to give in. Matthias is a fighter. He's a well-trained mercenary. He's willing to sacrifice himself before giving up that information. There's no way we're going to break him in time with the usual good cop bad cop routine," he said.

"So, what are you suggesting?" asked Mick. Ethan paused for a moment.

"I think we're going to have to push the boundaries of the interrogation."

"I don't follow?"

"Does Granger have a family here?" asked Ethan. The line paused for a moment.

"Just hold on a moment," said Mick. Ethan waited as Mick made his way across the main floor and approached Felicity's station. "Felicity, bring up Matthias Granger's personal profile. I need to find out if he's got any family here," he said.

"Got it." Felicity started typing away at her computer. Within a matter of seconds, she pulled up the intelligence file on Matthias Granger. It was access restricted and imported from ASIO. "Here it is...According to the Department of Defence, Matthias Granger has a wife and two children, a boy,

Aiden, and a girl. Chloe," said Felicity, as she read from the screen.

"Does DOD have an address on file?" asked Mick, as he too read over the screen.

"Hold on, checking," she said. She scanned the report. "Yes, they're renting a house through the housing commission located in Newport...25 Milford Street, Newport."

"Ethan, did you get any of that?"

"Yeah, I did. Thanks."

"I don't quite get where you're going with this," said Mick. Ethan didn't say anything, and then turned to look back at Matthias. He was staring at Ethan the whole time.

"Contact the Victorian Police...Have them detain Matthias' family," he said. Mick Greer didn't know how to respond to that.

"Jesus, Ethan. You can't be serious? That's kind of illegal. We can't just arrest innocent people. They're Australian citizens."

"Boss, they're not innocent. They are family of a high-profile criminal mastermind. We have a legal right to detain family members who have connections to terrorists," Ethan replied. Mick just let out a sigh.

"I just don't feel comfortable doing this. If it backfires, it could damage the agency's reputation," said Mick. Ethan let out a sigh.

"I know...I might have another way. I'll get back to you." Ethan hung up the phone. He thought for a second and then started dialling another number. It rang for a few times, but then someone finally picked up. "Hey, it's me. Are you still looking for work?" he asked. "I have a job for you…There's a family in Newport, Melbourne. They're family of a criminal we captured. He's refusing to give up critical information about a nuclear device. Think you could work your magic?" said Ethan. There was a slight pause as he waited for a response. Then, he made a grin. "Thank you. Call me when you're ready." He hung up and then walked over to Matthias. "You will tell us where that bomb is."

"I invite you to try, pig!" Matthias replied. Ethan just looked at him, not saying anything.

The digital clock timer was rapidly counting down. Adam Cochran was still sitting next to the dirty bomb. He sat there and watched as dozens of people walked by. They had no clue that their lives were in danger, or that a nuclear device was minutes away from detonating. The bomb's timer ticked on. 08:44:21…08:44:20…08:44:19.

Five minutes went by. Detective Sergeant Ethan Cooper knew he'd crossed the line with this, but it was the only way that he was going to get Matthias Granger to talk. Ethan was getting impatient as he waited for his contact in Melbourne to call back. While he waited, Sam Hunter came over and he carried a handheld tablet device. He placed it on a large box in front of Matthias and turned it on. Matthias just looked at him with a sinister grin on his face. He stood there staring at Matthias. Just then, Ethan's mobile started ringing. It rang a couple of times, but then he quickly answered it. "Ethan Cooper." It was his contact from Melbourne. "Good. We've got a Tablet device ready. Send us the video link," he requested. A few moments later, a video appeared on the Tablet. It was a live video stream and showed several men wearing balaclavas and were holding three people hostage in their own home. One of the hostiles was holding a knife against the throat of Matthias' wife, Melissa Granger. Matthias began to struggle in attempt to break free from his restraints.

"You fucking bastard pigs!" he shouted. "If you hurt my family, I'll fucking kill you!" he said, getting angry, and got red in the face. He was breathing quite rapidly. Ethan grinned at that, as it was the reaction he was hoping to get.

"This is how it's going to work, Granger…If you don't tell me where that bomb is, I'm going to start executing your family one by one, starting with your daughter, Chloe," he threatened. Matthias was getting angry. Sam stood by and was finding this whole experience quite overwhelming. He didn't know how to feel about all of this. "Tell me where the bomb is!" Ethan shouted, getting up close to Matthias' bloodied face. "Your operation is over, Granger. You might as well give up and save your family…Tell me where the bomb is!" again, Matthias refused to give in.

"Go to hell, pig!" he shouted, and spat out more blood. Ethan thought for a moment. He then took out his phone and hit the speed dial.

"It's me...Are you ready?" he asked. "Good...Take out the daughter," he requested. "You brought this on yourself, Granger!" Ethan grabbed hold of Matthias by the back of his head and forced him to watch the video. He could see one of Ethan's men walking up to Matthias' eight-year-old daughter, Chloe. The man had a silenced handgun and pointed it at the child's head. At the last second, the armed man pushed the chair over and fired a shot. Matthias screamed out in anger and started wailing.

"You son of a bitch!" he shouted. Sam couldn't believe what had happened.

"I just executed your daughter, Matthias! You have two more chances...Tell me where the bomb is, or I'll execute your son, it's your choice, Granger!" he said. Matthias was getting more frustrated, as he couldn't do anything to help his family. "I'm giving you five seconds...One...Two...Three...Four..." "You wouldn't dare," said Matthias. Ethan stared at him for a second. "Five...Take out the son," said Ethan. He was still on the line with his contact in Melbourne. Matthias' heart was racing, and his breathing increased. He saw the man on the video walking in front of Matthias' son. He had his gun aimed at the boy's head and was getting ready to pull the trigger. "You're running out of time, Matthias!" he shouted. Still, Matthias refused to give. "Take him out!" The armed man was preparing to take a shot at the boy.

"Wait! Wait! Stop!" Matthias called out. Finally, Ethan's plan worked, and Matthias cracked.

"Hold your fire," said Ethan. "Are you going to tell me where the bomb is?" he asked. Matthias slowly nodded. He literally broke down into tears. "Stand down, gents. I'll get back to you." Ethan hung up the phone. "Tell me where the bomb is!" Of course, Matthias didn't reply straight away. He was too distraught to even think about talking. "Start talking!"

"Okay…The bomb is in a blue van. It is parked in the city centre," he said.

"Where in the city centre?" again, Matthias hesitated to reply. "Where!?"

"Martin Place Station." Ethan's eyes widened. At that, he quickly dialled another number.

"Mick Greer."

"Hey Boss, it's me again. Matthias talked. He gave up the location of the dirty bomb."

"That's good news. Where is it?" he asked.

"It's at Martin Place Station. In a blue van. Is there a tactical unit nearby?"

"Yeah, I think so. I'll dispatch a unit. Diane Faulkner will be with them," he said.

"Okay good. Tell her to approach with caution, the van will probably be defended."

"Copy that."

At Martin Place station, more and more people were starting to congregate. It was approaching five o'clock in the afternoon, which meant it was peak hour. Many people were catching the train home from work. However, several of the train services had been delayed because of the terrorist attack on the Sydney Harbour Bridge. Adam Cochran was still sitting next to the dirty bomb. Its clock timer continued counting down. 03:04:22...03:04:21...03:04:20. SCU Detective Sergeant Diane Faulkner accompanied a counter-terrorist squad. They were in tight formation and quickly approached the rear end of the blue van. The group stopped about a hundred metres away and the officers readied their guns. "We're in position," said Diane Faulkner over her radio.

"Proceed with caution," Mick Greer responded. Then, Diane and the officers continued to walk towards the van. Onlookers were surprised to see the counter-terrorist soldiers advancing towards a vehicle. They got within twenty metres of the van. Adam heard a slight banging noise from the side of the van. It startled him. He looked through the rear-view mirror and sure enough, he spotted the tactical police officers. He started sweating. Reacting quickly, he took out his handgun, and loaded it. He looked over at the bomb's timer and it read: 02:01:49...02:01:48...02:01:47. He knew he had to keep the officers distracted for two more minutes, which wasn't going to be easy, but he had no choice. He pushed open one of the doors and started firing at the officers. Diane quickly ducked for cover. Luckily, the lead officer was holding a tactical police shield, and it collected a majority of the bullets. Adam continued firing and managed to injure one of the officers. As the officers were taking most of the hits, Diane advanced forward and managed to make her way over to the front. Carefully, she opened the passenger side door and climbed up.

"Drop the weapon!" Diane shouted. Adam stopped firing. "Drop it!" Adam paused for a moment. Instead of dropping the gun, he swung round and went to fire at Diane. But she responded first and fired a shot. It struck Adam in the shoulder, and he fell to the floor. Meanwhile, Diane's eyes widened as she saw the dirty bomb. The timer was counting down and ticked passed one minute. "Shit." 00:50:31…00:50:30…00:50:29. "How do I disarm the bomb?" she asked, pointing her gun at Adam. He was clutching his gunshot wound, and on the verge of passing out. "How do I disarm it?" She grabbed hold of him and pressed the nozzle of her gun against the wound. He yelped out in agonizing pain.

"Disarming code…1446552," he said, with a struggle. With shaking hands, Diane punched in the code on the number pad. She hit enter and the code was accepted. The bomb was disarmed, and its timer stopped at 00:10:02. She closed her eyes and sighed with relief. Then, she took out her mobile phone to dial a number.

"Mick Greer."

"Boss, it's Diane…The dirty bomb is secure. I repeat, the dirty bomb is secure," she said.

At the Carriage-works warehouse, Ethan Cooper was standing around waiting to hear from the SCU. Sam was standing there, and he too was starting to get worried about the whole situation. Matthias Granger was sitting in the chair still hand cuffed with several officers watching over him. They were both armed with assault rifles. Ethan stood there waiting patiently. Just then, his phone started ringing. "Detective Cooper," he answered.

"Ethan, it's me...The bomb is secure." Ethan sighed with relief.

"Thank God. Thanks Boss, we're bringing in Matthias," said Ethan and then he hung up. With a satisfied look, he put away his phone. As he went to walk over to Sam who was talking with a couple of officers, he was stopped as Matthias called out to him.

"Detective Cooper," he said. "There's something you need to know…About your friend, Detective Simon Harper." Ethan paused and slowly turned around.

"What are you talking about?" he asked, as he came over to him.

"He's not who he says he is…He is a traitor," said Matthias. Ethan's eyes widened at that.

"Why the fuck should I believe you?" he said. Matthias didn't reply straight away.

"My operation was funded by Carmichael Enterprises," he began. "They were also sub-contracted by Birchall McClelland…My employer was Karl Benedict." Ethan's eyes widened as he heard that name. "He financed this entire operation and allowed me and my men to steal the radioactive material," he added. Ethan was just speechless.

"What does Simon have to do with this?" Matthias didn't reply straight away.

"After I met with Mr. Benedict, he told me that we would be given assistance by someone in the federal police. Someone who we could gather information from and monitor the police's movements…Simon Harper is that person. He warned us that you were coming to arrest me," he said. Ethan didn't know how to respond at that. He was furious and could not believe what he was hearing. "You must believe me...I have no reason to lie, you killed my family. I am telling you this out of honesty," he replied. Ethan closed his eyes. At that, Sam came over.

"Everything alright?" he asked. Ethan didn't say anything at first.

"Yeah, I just spoke with SCU. The dirty bomb is secure," he said.

"Oh, thank God...So it's over?" asked Sam, and Ethan slowly nodded.

"Yeah...By the way, have you got Matthias' phone there?" said Ethan.

"I think so, it's here. Why?"

"I just need to check it." Sam gave it to him and he opened it up. He scrolled through the recently called numbers. There were a lot of different numbers that appeared on the screen, but as he moved down the list, one of the numbers jumped out at him. His eyes lit up and he couldn't believe it. "Ethan, what's wrong?" asked Sam. Ethan was just frozen in shock.

President of Australia, Christine Mills was in her office at the Government House. It had been a long day for Christine and she was still feeling rather emotional about the events of the day. She was still finding it overwhelming at the fact that terrorists managed to carry out an attack on the Sydney Harbour Bridge. She also couldn't believe that she had just found out that her Official Secretary, Joe Parsons, had paid someone to abduct a nationally recognized journalist in attempt to keep him from publishing a major story; but she had no choice and had to go through with it. Christine sat at her desk, and pondered through some overdue paperwork, and was trying to decide what she should do regarding Joe. As she worked, the TV was on and it showed a news report and recaptured the day's events. As she sat there watching, there was a knock at the door. Moments later, Joe Parsons entered. Christine muted the TV. She was still angry at him for what he did. "Good evening, Your Excellency. How are you feeling?" he asked, closing the door.

"Hi Joe. Yes, I'm okay, just exhausted to be honest," she said, and Joe slowly nodded.

"I can understand that…I just got off the phone with Chief Inspector Mick Greer from the Serious Crimes Unit…He informed me that the dirty bomb has been secured," said Joe.

"Oh, Joe that is the best news I've heard all day," she said, and Joe smiled.

"Yes, I thought you'd be happy with that…He also said that all hostiles involved with the terrorist plot have been detained."

"Good…I want to make a statement as soon as possible."

"I'll set it up." As Joe was about to leave, he was stopped.

"Joe, there's one more thing," she said. Joe closed the door and turned back.

"What's that, Your Excellency?" Christine didn't say anything at first.

"Joe...After the day's events, I've decided that I cannot continue to serve as head of state. Therefore, I will be officially announcing my intention to resign the office of the President in a special session of parliament tomorrow," she said. Joe was completely shocked.

"Your Excellency, if I may, I believe you're making a huge mistake," he said, but Christine just shook her head.

"No, Joe. It's not a mistake...I crossed the line when I paid off that journalist," she said. "I'm not that person, Joe. I put the faith and trust in the Australian people and I betrayed that trust," she said. Joe didn't know what to say to that.

"We can fix this, Christine. There's only a small group of people who know about this," said Joe.

"No. If one of those people breaks this story, then this government will be thrown into chaos," she said. "I will be officially making the announcement tomorrow morning." Joe couldn't believe it.

"Ma'am, I don't know what to say...I feel responsible for your decision," said Joe. Christine shook her head.

"It's not your fault, Joe. One way or another, I'd end up having to resign anyway. My Parkinson's Disease is getting worse every day...It's better I leave now, rather than further down the track, especially with an election year coming up next year," she said.

"That's true, I still feel bad for you." Christine didn't say anything. She just smiled. The room fell silent for a moment.

"Is there anything I can do for you?" he asked. Christine let out a sigh.

"I need you to set up a conference call with the Chairman of the APSC. I'm going to inform him of my decision to step down," she said, and Joe nodded. "I also want to contact the Prime Minister. He needs to know what's going on," she said. The room fell silent after that.

Chief Inspector Mick Greer was in his office. He was so pleased that the crisis was over, and that the dirty bomb was now secured. He was also relieved that the terrorist behind the bomb attack on the Sydney Harbour Bridge, Matthias Granger, was in custody. It was approaching five o'clock in the afternoon, and it was almost time to knock off home after a long, hard day. There was still a few more things to do yet, but it wouldn't be long before he was able to leave. He had a stack of paperwork to finish off and sign. As he was sitting there, the TV was on and it was showing a reporter giving an update on the bombing of the Harbour Bridge. Currently, Mick was talking on the phone. He was talking to Chief Superintendent Anna Mackenzie, who was on her way back from Canberra. She was pleased with how well Mick and the task force operated today. As he spoke, there was a knock at his door. Mick looked up to see that it was Simon Harper. "Yes, I can confirm that the dirty bomb is secure, and Matthias Granger has been taken into custody," said Mick.

Simon's heart started racing as he heard that. "Of course, I'll brief you when you get here." Then Mick hung up. "Detective Harper, what can I do for you?"

"What was that about?"

"Just updating the Chief Superintendent. She's on her way back from Canberra. You'll get to meet her in the next hour," said Mick.

"Great. Can't wait," he replied, sarcastically, and Mick chuckled. "Did I hear you just say that Matthias Granger was captured?"

"Yes. Ethan and the tactical unit raided the warehouse. He and his cell members were taken down. Matthias Granger is being transported in as we speak," said Mick. Simon started to get a bit worried.

"I see, well that's good news. And the dirty bomb was secure?" he asked. Mick looked up, confused.

"Yes. The Army took control of it. It's being taken to Holsworthy Army Base for dismantling," said Mick. "This will all be in your debrief report tomorrow, Detective." Simon just nodded.

"I'm aware of that, and I just wanted to say that I won't be coming in tomorrow," he replied.

"I don't follow?" Simon handed Mick an envelope.

"I'm handing in my letter of resignation, effective immediately," he said. Mick was somewhat confused by all of this.

"I'm not sure I understand what's going on. Why are you resigning? Have you spoken with Ethan about this?"

"It's part of the reason why I'm resigning, Sir. I feel that we can't continue to work together. We had a disagreement five years ago, and frankly, it still feels like it happened yesterday," said Simon. "I just don't want the SCU to have to worry about something like this." Mick was speechless.

"I don't know what to say…Are you sure you're making the right decision?" he asked. Simon slowly nodded.

"Yes. It's for the best. I don't want to be a burden to you or your office," he said. Mick stood up and reached out his hand.

"Well, I appreciate all your hard work, Simon. It's been a privilege to have had you on the team," he said, and they shook hands.

"It's no problem. I appreciate you taking me on…Now, if you'll excuse me, I think there's a stiff drink waiting for me at the local pub," he said, and Mick laughed.

"Have one for me, why don't you?" he said, and Simon nodded. Then he turned and headed out the door.

There was certainly a lot going through Ethan Cooper's mind. He just couldn't believe that his best friend, Simon Harper was working for the terrorists. He felt betrayed and angry by Simon's treachery. Ethan was driving in the Range Rover Sports vehicle and was making his way back to the SCU. It was night time and just on eleven o'clock at night. There were not that many cars on the road which made his trip quick. As he drove towards the city, he took out his phone to dial a number. "Chief Inspector Greer," Mick answered.

"Hey, it's me...Are you alone?" he asked. Mick paused and looked around her.

"Yes, what's going on Ethan?"

"Look, there's something I need to talk to you about. It's not going to be easy for you to hear, but believe me, it's the truth," he said.

"Ethan, what's going on? You're scaring me," he said. Ethan didn't know how to respond.

"Simon Harper is working for the terrorists," he said. The line just went dead quiet.

"Ethan, that is ridiculous. I just had Simon in my office. He resigned by the way, because you two had a high-school rowel five years ago...Simon was a good detective, and a value to the task force," said Mick.

"Son of a bitch...He made that up. I never had an argument with him. We've been best friends for ten years. He was trying to make an excuse, so you'd accept his resignation. I found out that Simon called Matthias' phone multiple times throughout the day...It's definitely his number, Boss." Mick let out a sigh. He was having trouble trying to understand what was being said.

"There's got to be another explanation."

"No, there isn't. He's part of this terrorist conspiracy...Look, I'm on my way back to the office. You can't let Simon leave the building. Just trust me on this, Boss...Simon is a traitor, and if Matthias gave him up, then

Simon knows his cover's been blown. He's trying to make a run for it," said Ethan. There was a sudden pause in the conversation.

"What is it you want me to do?" asked Mick.

"I don't want you to do anything that will alarm him. He's not expecting you to know he's been exposed, just act normally. Where is he now?"

"I think he's on his way out the door, Ethan. He just handed me his resignation, then he was going to the pub."

"Son of a bitch…Okay, call security. Tell them to detain Simon but tell them to approach him with caution. I'll be there in five minutes."

"Okay, fine. Get here fast."

Simon Harper was already in the elevator. He was making his way down to the underground parking garage. He was annoyed because he just heard the conversation between Ethan Cooper and Mick Greer. He'd been listening in on them talking and knew his cover had been blown. He knew he had to prepare to leave as he could not afford to be captured. He stood there in the elevator, he took out his phone to dial a number. The call rang for a few moments and then it finally connected. "Yes?" a voice answered.

"Mr. Benedict, it's Simon Harper," he said. There was a sudden pause.

"What can I do for you, Mr. Harper?"

"Matthias Granger spilled the beans about my involvement…Ethan Cooper is on his way, he knows I warned Granger," said Simon.

"That's disappointing, Simon. How did this happen?"

"I told you, it was Matthias. He couldn't keep his God damn mouth shut. If Ethan Cooper gets his hands on me, you know he'll make me talk," said Simon.

"Then you'd better make sure that doesn't happen," said Karl.

"You know what you have to do." Simon didn't reply straight away, as he knew what he was talking about. Then the call disconnected. The elevator continued to descend, and as it did, Simon lifted his wrist and pressed a button on the side of his digital watch.

Upon doing so, he had activated the timer on a bomb which Simon had planted within the building. It was his insurance policy to make sure that he could get away if his cover was ever blown. The timer on the bomb was set for two minutes, and it began counting down. Simon's watch was synchronized with the bomb's timer, so he knew exactly how much time he had to leave. Ethan Cooper was focusing on his driving. He was behind the wheel of the SCU Range Rover Sports and heading towards the SCU building. There was a lot going through his mind, and he was utterly distraught at the fact that Simon Harper was a traitor. He and Simon were very close and went on many missions in the SASR. He wasn't caring that he'd driven past several red lights, he just wanted to get back to the office before Simon left. As he continued driving, his Blue tooth started buzzing. Ethan connected the call.

"Detective Cooper."

"Ethan. How far away are you?" It was Mick Greer.

"I'm thirty seconds out. Any sign of Simon?" he asked.

"No. CCTV picked him up heading to the parking garage. He should be there by now."

"Okay, I'm almost there. Just make sure the security teams are ready," said Ethan, and then hung up. He then put his foot down harder on the accelerator. He was closing in on the SCU office.

Simon Harper was in the elevator. He was starting to panic as it seemed to be taking forever. But that was probably because he knew he was about to be caught. Finally, the elevator arrived, and he made his way across the parking garage towards his car. As he was about to climb into the front seat, he looked up as he heard the screeching tires of a car pulling in. It was Ethan Cooper. He was driving straight toward Simon's parked car and rammed straight into it. The force of the crash knocked Simon to the ground. Ethan climbed out of the car and ran over to him with his gun raised. "Put your hands out!" Ethan shouted. "Do it!" Simon was still a bit shaken by the impact of the car. "Put your hands up above your head, now!" he yelled. Slowly, Simon put his hands forward. A few moments later, a group of tactical officers came charging over. Ethan cuffed Simon and dragged him up so that he was face to face. "You're a son of a bitch, Simon!" he said. Simon had a cut on his forehead and he was sweating.

"Go to hell, Cooper," he said. Ethan pressed his gun against Simon's forehead and held his finger on the trigger. He was certainly ready to fire. But as he was about to, he was stopped as Mick Greer came over.

"Detective Cooper, lower your weapon!" he shouted. At first, Ethan didn't respond and continued to hold the gun at Simon's face. "Detective Cooper, put down the gun, now, or so help me God I will put you down," Mick threatened. Ethan hesitated, but he had no choice but to surrender.

"You'll never win, Cooper…I'll always be better than you," he said. Ethan just stood there, with an angry expression on his face. He wanted nothing more than to bash him up, but he was being held by several officers. "By the way, I have a backup plan." Ethan's eyes widened at that.

"What are you talking about?"

"You know what I'm talking about, Cooper. I always have a backup plan." Ethan realised what he was talking about. He looked over him, and then spotted his watch. He grabbed his wrist and turned it over. Ethan's eyes widened as he saw the digital timer counting down.

"Son of a bitch!" he cursed.

"What is it, Ethan?" asked Mick, looking confused.

"There's a bomb in the building. You need to evacuate everyone, now!" Ethan said, in a raised voice.

"Bloody hell. How much time do we have?"

"Less than sixty seconds...Where's the bomb, you bastard?" he demanded, as he took hold of Simon's neck. He began to squeeze.

"It's not going to work that way, Cooper," he said, with a struggle. Ethan was angry. He wanted to squeeze so badly and make him choke to death.

"Damn it!" Ethan yelled.

"Get everybody out, now!" he said. At that, the tactical police officers scattered and immediately conducted an evacuation. But it was too late. Seconds went by, and the bomb exploded.

12 Hours Later.

Christine Mills was tired. She couldn't believe what had happened over the past twenty-four-hours and that there was an attack on the Sydney Harbour Bridge. It was all over the news and most of the morning talk shows were talking about it. She was currently in her office at the Government House in Canberra. She was standing by the window and gazing out at the yard, watching as the sun rose. It was a bright orange, red colour with a hint of grey from the clouds. As she stood there in deep thought, the TV was on and it was currently displaying a news update on the bombing. It also stated that federal police thwarted a potential terrorist attack involving a radiological explosive device. Of course, she didn't pay much attention to it, because she already knew it was happening. She had a cup of coffee on the desk which had been sitting there for the past half an hour and was probably cold by now. Just then, there was a knock at the door. She didn't respond, and it opened. Joe Parsons, her Official Secretary stepped in. It had been a long night, and Joe was feeling pretty tired. "Good morning, Your Excellency," he said. She didn't reply straight away, and she looked over.

"Oh, morning, Joe. What's happening?" she asked, finally.

"I've just spoken with the Speaker of the House. He's authorized a special session of parliament," said Joe, and Christine nodded.

"Very good. I'll head over there shortly," she said. There was a brief pause in the conversation. Joe stood there and watched as she sat back down.

"Ma'am, I really think you're making a big mistake," he said. Of course, Christine shook her head.

"No, Joe, we've been over this...I chose to cover up this illness. I agreed to blackmail a journalist and prevent him from exposing the truth...I need to tell the people the truth," she said. Joe just stood there for a moment and didn't say anything. Just then, there was a knock at the door. It was Christine's Executive Assistant, Brian Stedman.

"Excuse me, Your Excellency...Your car is ready out front," said Brian, and she smiled.

"Thanks Brian." She then got up and put on her jacket. "Thanks for all your help Joe, you've done a wonderful job," she said. Joe smiled. He stood there and watched as Christine headed to the door.

After a ten-minute drive from the residence, the President of Australia, Christine Mills, had arrived at the Parliament House. There was a lot going through her mind as the presidential state car, a Range Rover Sports Executive, pulled into the underground parking garage. It was a space reserved strictly for parliamentary staff and members of parliament. The vehicle pulled into the President's designated parking space and it sat there for a moment as Christine sat there day dreaming. She was in deep thought and thinking back to the day when she was chosen to be the President of Australia. "We're here, Your Excellency," said Joe, as he was sitting in the seat next to Christine. She didn't reply straight away, until Joe placed his hand on her shoulder. She then jumped. "Are you okay?"

"Ah, yes, sorry Joe...Let's get this over with," she replied. Then the door opened, and Christine climbed out. Christine was then escorted into the Parliament House. She was about to announce her resignation in a speech in a special session of parliament in front of the Prime Minister and the entire House of Representatives. Christine was escorted down a long corridor with Joe Parsons accompanying her, along with several other officials, and the President's security detail. She approached a glass door and imprinted on it was; 'HOUSE OF

REPRESENTATIVES'. She paused before opening it and let out a sigh.

"Are you sure about this, Ma'am?" asked Joe. She didn't reply straight away, and slowly nodded.

"Yes." She then pushed open the door and went in. She walked down a short corridor before the set of double doors were opened for her. These doors led into the House of Representatives' chambers, the centre of government of the Republic of Australia. "Mr. Speaker, Mr. Prime Minister...The President of the Republic of Australia!" a voice spoke, as Christine entered. Everyone in the chambers stood up from their seats and immediately started clapping, as Christine made her way down to the centre platform. The standing ovation lasted for about five minutes, and Christine spent that time shaking hands with members.

Eventually, she finally made it to the front bench, where she shook hands with the Prime Minister and Deputy Prime Minister. She then shook hands with the Speaker and took his seat to give her speech. Christine was nervous at first, mostly because she was about to give her resignation. She then let out a deep breath and prepared herself to speak.

"Mr. Speaker, Mr. Prime Minister, fellow members of parliament," she began. "Yesterday, this nation was struck by a terrible tragedy...Our way of life was threatened when terrorists carried out an attack on the Sydney Harbour Bridge, which resulted in the loss of more than a hundred innocent people," she said. There was an eerie moment of silence. "I come before you, the members of parliament, to inform you that as a result of exceptional management and effortless work by the Australian Federal Police in Sydney, the terrorist behind those atrocities, is now in custody and awaiting trial for his heinous crimes," said Christine. At that, the chambers erupted into an applause. After they all settled down, Christine continued to speak. "Thank you...I'd like to offer my sincere gratitude to the brave men and women who worked tirelessly and who risked their lives during the course of the investigation," she said. There was another brief applause. "Now, I realise this is an awkward time, however...I would like to announce that I, Christine Mills, will be officially stepping down as President of the Republic of Australia," she said. There was a lot of indistinctive chatter amongst the members of parliament, as they were shocked by the President's sudden decision. "I regret this decision, however, due to some unfortunate health concerns, I believe I am unfit to continue to serve as the nations' head of state...I hereby tender my resignation, as President of this country, effective immediately," said Christine. No one said at first, and then they slowly began to clap. Christine smiled, and she began heading out. She shook hands with everyone again and walked towards the door.

It had been a long, emotional day for the Serious Crimes Unit. They were still dealing with the aftermath of the terrorist attack on the Harbour Bridge, as well as the unexpected bomb explosion at the SCU office in Sydney. The explosion was massive. It'd taken out most of the SCU building and resulted in more than forty deaths. Dozens more were seriously injured, including Felicity Meyers, and Sam Hunter. For hours after the explosion, emergency responders were attempting to distinguish the flames, and tried to search for more survivors. Thankfully, Ethan Cooper and Mick Greer made it out of the building before the explosion. Simon Harper also made it out alive, much to Ethan's disappointment. He wanted to leave him there, and die in the explosion, but he knew that wasn't going to be an option. Ethan knew Simon would have valuable intelligence. After the explosion, Ethan and Mick were transported to Canberra, along with Simon Harper. They were transferred to the AFP's headquarters building.

The AFP Headquarters was the Edmund Barton Building, and named after Edmund Barton, Australia's first Prime Minister. SCU Chief Inspector Mick Greer walked through the main entrance of the AFP building. After clearing through security, he headed up the stairs to the main operations centre. This was his second time here and he was still overwhelmed by the size of the place. He was still covered with dust from the explosion, but he didn't care. Mick climbed the stairs, exhausted, and knocked on the glass door to the office of Anna Mackenzie, the Chief Superintendent.

She'd been at the headquarters the whole time but was keeping up to date with everything that'd happened. "Jesus,

Mick. You look like crap," Anna said, stating the obvious, but she was being sarcastic.

"Good of you to notice, Anna…I see you're quite comfortable in this large, spacious office," Mick replied. Anna didn't say anything, she just chuckled. There was a TV on in the office and it was showing a news report on the bomb explosion at the SCU.

"I have to admit, I was quite shocked when I heard about the explosion at the SCU…I'd like to know how it happened," she said. Mick let out a sigh, and sat down, taking a sip of water. His throat was dry and sore from the inhalation of dust.

"Emergency response are still assessing the situation. But, it was Simon Harper…He planted the device. It was his backup plan of escape." Anna closed her eyes in disappointment. The room fell silent after that.

"What's happening with Detective Harper now?" she asked, changing the subject.

"He's being taken to one of the holding rooms. I'm just about to go and question him," said Mick, and Anna nodded. Mick got up and headed to the door. As he went to open it, he was stopped as Anna called out.

"By the way, Mick…I was reviewing the transcripts from the operation to capture Matthias Granger," she said.

"Oh yes, and?"

"I noticed that Matthias gave up the location of the dirty bomb, but from what I recall, Detective Cooper informed you that Mr. Granger wasn't going to break in time," she said. "I'd like to know how Cooper managed to get him to give up the bomb's location?" asked Anna. There was a brief pause. Mick let out a sigh and looked back at Anna.

"He got the information through a special means...He used Granger's family as leverage," he said.

"Yes, I saw the footage of the act...This is totally unacceptable, Mick. You should have stopped him," she said.

"I did, Anna. But you know what Ethan's like, he did it on his own accord, against my authority," said Mick.

"I still don't like what he did, Mick. It goes against everything the AFP stands for."

"Chief Superintendent, if I may...If it wasn't for Ethan, tens of thousands of people would have been killed if that dirty bomb detonated," said Mick. Anna didn't reply, and she continued staring at Mick.

"I agree, but I still don't approve of what he did...I'm giving him a verbal warning. The next time he does something like this, he's to be suspended," she said, and Mick nodded. He grabbed the door handle.

"I'll make sure to tell him," said Mick, and then he walked out. Anna just sat there, watching. After Simon's arrest, he was placed in one of HQ's holding rooms. A security guard had been placed outside the door.

Detective Sergeant Ethan Cooper was standing in the observation room and stared at Simon through the double-sided window. He stood there for a good five minutes, thinking about how angry he was that Simon was a traitor.

They had been friends for more than twenty or so years, and even went through High School together. He just didn't think that Simon was the type to be a traitor. He wanted nothing more than to walk into the room and kill Simon. As he stood there watching, the door opened. Ethan looked over to see Mick Greer enter. He didn't look happy, which is understandable.

"Hey Boss. Wasn't expecting to see you," said Ethan.

"I know. I was just being grilled by Mackenzie. She wasn't happy at the fact that Simon Harper was a traitor, and that he managed to infiltrate the agency," he said, and Ethan rolled his eyes.

"Has he said anything yet?" he asked.

"Not yet. He's only just arrived, and we've been sweating him." There was a brief pause in the conversation. "What's the latest with Sydney?"

"So far, forty dead, twenty-two seriously wounded," he explained, and Ethan closed his eyes.

"Son of a bitch."

"Felicity is in an induced coma. Sam's undergoing surgery. Diane's getting minor surgery on her arm," said Mick.

"I can't believe this…Boss, we can't let this psychopath get away with this. He has to pay for what he's done!" Ethan shouted, getting frustrated.

"I know Ethan and he will. But we have to question him first. If he was involved with the terrorists, then there's a good chance that he has valuable Intel," he said. Ethan just shook his head.

"I want to be the one to question him."

"No, absolutely not. Ethan, he was your best friend who turned out to be a traitor, I can't let you in that room. Mackenzie agrees too, she's forbidden you to come face to face with Simon Harper," he explained. Mick just shook his head.

"Still, you endangered the lives of three innocent people."
"I realise that, Boss. But I did what I had to in order to find that dirty bomb. Because of what I did, tens of thousands of innocent lives were spared," he said. Mick didn't reply straight away. He wasn't impressed by what he did, but he knew he did the right thing.

"I spoke with Mackenzie about what happened…She wasn't particularly pleased with what you did, but, she's prepared to overlook it for you one time only. Let this be a warning to you…This is not the Special Air Service Regiment. We do not threaten lives," he said, and Ethan nodded.

"Understood." The room fell silent after that. Mick looked back at Simon Harper who was still sitting at the table.

"I still can't believe he's a traitor…I've known him for ten years, I never would have suspected him as a criminal."

"What's going to happen to him?" Mick looked down at his watch. He thought for a moment before replying.

"Mackenzie has spoken with the Commissioner regarding this. It's likely Simon will be charged with conspiracy to aid a terrorist organization. He will end up going to prison for the rest of his life," he said. Ethan didn't know what to say to that. "Good work today, Ethan, apart from the situation with Granger. Now, finish up your debrief, and then you're free to go home for the day," said Mick. He then went over to open the door to enter the interview room. Ethan stood there for a moment and watched as Mick sat down at the table to talk to Mick.

He then made his way out of the observation room. He got into the elevator and it took him down to the agency's underground carpark. His car was parked a few hundred metres away. Slowly, he walked over to it and climbed into the driver's side. He sat there for a moment and turned on the ignition. But before he drove off, he took a moment to think about what had happened in the past twenty-four hours or so. He started to feel emotional and distraught by the fact that his best friend, Simon Harper, was a criminal. The stress of the day's events finally caught up with him and he broke down into tears. He also thought about his wife, Susan, as it was recently the anniversary of her passing. He missed her so much every day and wished it never happened. After breaking down, he put the car into gear and then drove off.

THE END